Dedication

To my husband Don (Six), thank you for loving me and believing in my dreams. You are a wonderful husband and I love you with all my heart.

To my children, Ashley and Avien my Godchildren, Dominique and De'Jene and my granddaughters A'yana, MaKenzi and Maddison. I challenge you all to follow your dreams. Take the Lord with you in all your endeavors and He will help you reach your goals. I love you all.

To my best friend Shirelle, you have been a sister to me all my life. I love you with all my heart. Our paths were pre-written by God, it's no coincidence.

To my cousin Tami, I have always looked up to you. You have always been there for me when I needed you. Thanks for listening to the story over and over and over. Love cuz. "Rack em!"

To Robert Brooks and Dorothy Vance, thanks for being my proofreaders and my true friends. I can't wait to send the second book.

For my family and friends, I hope you enjoy reading this as much as I enjoyed writing it. To my Behr, Chipotle, Franks and church family, thank you for your support my love extends to all of you.

Acknowledgements

The Lord is my Savior and strength; I give Him all the praise and glory. I thank Him for giving me the talent of writing, and a creative imagination.

To my parents Tom and Georgia Davis, thank you both for being supportive and positive vessels in my life. Without you I couldn't have made it this far. I love you.

COVER DESIGN: AMB BRANDING DESIGN
www.ambbrandingdesign.com

To order additional copies of this book, contact:

shauntakenerly.wix.com/shaunta-presents
shauntakenerly@yahoo.com

Please leave a review

Sweatin'
by Miss Kim

Book Overview

Danielle Thompson, 23, single mother with high ambitions to be a writer and store owner, has a full proof plan to get just what she wants. Taking a job at a greeting card store, Dani quickly becomes the protégé and best friend of her boss Mrs. Cheryl.

Everything was going her way until the man she's loved all her life "changes his mind" about their relationship.

Vowing to never let a man hurt her again, Dani loves'em and leaves'em and engulfs herself in work. However, Dani accepts an offer to attend a conference on a tropical Island for both business and relaxation from her boss. Lasting friendships are formed and an unspoken jealousy arises between boss and employee. Dani's life is changed forever.

With all that is going on around her, Dani manages to put the past behind her and open up to the man she would marry. But will he stay with her after he finds out she is not who she says she is and is the number one suspect in a murder investigation?

Do you know how you affect people? Are you aware that the words and actions of your everyday life affect someone whether you know it or not? Of course there are many people we can name that have affected us all, such as Martin Luther King, Oprah Winfrey, and most recently, Barack Obama. The one thing they have in common is they are all positive influences. Are all our actions positive? Probably not.

We as common folk are not positive all of the time. In fact, we tend to seek the negative, finding fault in everything. We don't examine our words or actions carefully. We go about our day speaking and behaving the way we wish not considering the consequences they may have on someone, anyone, a stranger, even family.

In troubled times we ask ourselves, what did I do to deserve this? Why is this happening to me? Do we go back and analyze exactly what got us to this point? Most of the time it's our own fault life brings so much trials and tribulations. If we are totally honest, we know exactly what got us to this point; we just don't want to admit it or we are ashamed of it.

We are all human, and sometimes, we don't act or speak the best way we know we should. But what do we do when those same actions or words come back to haunt us? Own up to it and stay true to ourselves or do nothing and hope for the best.

What will Danielle Thompson do? Will she come clean of past indiscretions? Or will her past continue to threaten and haunt her and those closest to her.

Miss Kim

The employees of Reeds Greeting Cards agreed to meet at the Salem Avenue Applebee's to celebrate my one year anniversary of employment at the store. The waitress pulls two tables together to seat us, closing the blinds slightly, so the sunlight won't blind everyone. The aroma of ribs and French fries permeate the air, the buzzing of conversations, and orders being served and prepared rang loud throughout the restaurant. It's four o'clock in the evening, and we made it for happy hour. There was a nice crowd dining and all the hanging televisions are on sports channels. It seems all of the male patrons are seated in view of one.

Joining me is Nadine Hughes, Anthony the security guard, and Sakoya Powell. Sakoya sits next to me as I, Danielle Thompson is the main attraction. I had to make sure I was proper for this occasion. I splurged on myself and purchased a vintage, dark brown halter dress with open back, floor length with a deep v-neck for my ample bosom to both tease the flat-chest hater while tantalizing every man in my path. I added just a touch of Usher perfume so I smelled as good as I looked. I left both my heels and purse in the trunk of my car. I'm most comfortable in my matching brown ballet shoes.

"Hey boo, I see you looking hot! Oooh I wish I was as tall as you, so I could borrow that dress, hell all of your clothes! When did you get this? Is that you smelling like that? What kind of perfume is that? I know I can borrow that." Sakoya is rattling off a thousand questions at a time.

Sakoya talks extremely fast, it's very hard for me or anyone to get a word in. I often translate for people who cannot understand her. It truly gets

7

under my skin, but she gives great advice; she's a loyal best friend. While she awaits her prince charming to sweep her off her feet, she works at Saint Elizabeth Hospital as a Nurse's Aid.

Her mission in life is to find a man that will take care of her. Since we were young, her dreams always include the husband, two children (boy first then girl…like she has a say so in the matter), and the picket fence. Sakoya and I have been friends since kindergarten; she never misses an opportunity to tell everyone how we met.

"I got this the other…"

"Who is that?" Sakoya is trying to be as discreet as possible. Letting her long golden-brown, micro braids fall over her face providing a shield, so no one could hear the inquiry.

"This is what I'm talkin' 'bout…" I knew Sakoya would start as soon as a man showed up.

"Shhhh! See…I was trying to be nice and whisper. You all loud. He probably heard you."

"So! He ain't nobody anyway! He ain't shit so keep looking."

We're still waiting for the boss, Mrs. Cheryl, to arrive. This is all her idea, but Nadine set the wheels in motion. This is the first anniversary party Mrs. Cheryl has had for any employee. Although they are happy for me, they are also curious.

"What's really going on? We ain't never had an anniversary party, not even for Mrs. B., she's been here way longer than you." Anthony is always starting mess. Mrs. B. our cashier couldn't make it to party.

"There's a first time for everything, right?" I can tell by Anthony's reaction, he isn't satisfied with my answer. He lives to piss me off.

Miss Kim

"Aye, where yo dude at? Or should I say where yo girl at?" Anthony looks at me with a smirk.

Anthony sticks a fresh toothpick in his mouth. I saw him grab a handful on the way in. It's obvious he is jealous of my man Frederick, because he *is* my boyfriend. He accuses me of "brown nosing" Mrs. Cheryl. I don't care what he thinks, whatever it takes to get ahead. Once I'm on top, we'll see who's clutching my coattails.

"Please go somewhere boy! I'm going to have a good time, this is *my* party! You know you want me on your team, ain't gon happ'n, capt'n. What you can do since you all in my grill? Go get me a drink, make yourself useful, chop chop." I can dish it just like he can.

Anthony doesn't pay me attention when I'm in diva mode, he's so cool (at least he thinks) he just sits back twirling his toothpick looking at me. We always engage in playful banter; we make each other laugh, but he really does get on my last nerve.

"They got waitresses for that." Anthony retorts quickly.

Our waitress walked up as if on his cue, "May I take your orders?"

Fast talking Sakoya speaks first, ready to get the party started, "I'll have two Long Islands, thank you top shelf."

Nadine and Anthony look at her in amazement, like she really *is* trying to get the party started.

"Y'all remember my best friend, Sakoya right?" I introduced my friend. The two were staring at the long nailed, braid wearing fast talking friend.

"I ain't that crazy, one is for my girl! Ya'll

know we have been friends since kindergarten, right?" Sakoya is ready to tell the story.

My mind flashed back to all the school bus rides together, all the notes we passed in class, senior skip day, and the time I used black eyeliner pencil to cover a bald spot in Sakoya's head because she tried to cut layers in her hair. The flashback is interrupted by the ringing of my cell phone, "Hello?"

"Your daughter and I just got in not too long ago. She's already playing dress up in my old dresses. You should see her," Stephani, my older sister says on the other end.

"What did you buy today? More stuff for the nursery Stephani?"

My sister, God bless her, needs therapy. She wants a baby so bad, but her husband Brandon, the work-a-holic, doesn't think it's the right time, but she still decided to decorate the room across from their bedroom into a nursery.

"There is nothing wrong with being prepared, right? Dad always says that's half the battle, right?" Stephani tries to justify.

"Whatever Stephani, you know you're not pregnant, *right*? I'll talk to you about this later, okay? Take a picture of my angel and send it to me." I hung up and continued drinking with my buddies.

Stephani is two years older yet everyone thinks I'm the oldest; it drives her crazy. I think because we are exact opposites. I am more aggressive, and she's passive. I wear make up, and she doesn't. I'm taller with long, beautiful scratch-free legs. She's slightly shorter with tomboy scars. Her bra size is an "A" cup, whereas my cup runneth over with ample breasts. I flaunt them often in front of her, so she feels threatened me by saying she's going to have a breast augmentation. I tell her that's on her, but she still won't measure up. We are very competitive with each other, but if it's us against someone, we will annihilate them. We do have that in common along with our jet black shoulder length hair and matching bracelet tattoos on our right wrists. I got mine first.

Nadine stands up with her big belly and almost knocks all the drinks over.

"Oh, I'm sorry. I have to go to the little ladies room."

Nadine waddles away. She is wearing a cute little sun dress, cut above the knee with a flower print. Her Jessica Simpson wedge heels show her well sculpted calves. She walks on her days off, so she won't gain too much weight. She's terrified of being overweight after the baby. The glow of pregnancy agrees with the flawless, tanned skinned, Nadine. Checking herself in the mirror, the door opened.

"Hey are you okay in here?" I had to go check on her.

"Oh yeah sweetie, I was on my way out. Are you having a good time? I think Anthony wants you for real. "

"See this is what I'm talkin' 'bout, girl why? You know Frederick has my heart."

"I know, I know sweetie, but you should give him a chance. I think you two make a cute couple. I gotta go, I was trying to stay around for Mrs. Cheryl but you know I gotta get back to the other side of town before you know who gets home. Give her a hug for me and I'll see ya'll Monday. I'll call you later." Nadine was out the door.

"Okay I'll tell'em... Yeah call me."

We all know why Nadine has to get home before her boyfriend does. He's having a hard time dealing with the thought of a new baby. He blames Nadine for getting pregnant. Stewart was totally happy with their family as is, Nadine, their two boys and him.

Back at the tables Sakoya and Anthony are doing shots of Tequila while onlookers from the other tables are trying not to watch.

"Aye girl, you're late. You gotta take two shots," Anthony hands me the Tequila filled shot glass. I notice his fingernails were nice, well shaped, no dirt.

See this is why I nicknamed him "yuck mouth." He doesn't know how to talk to a woman. He thinks he's being sexy but really it's just sad. He also has a pullout gold tooth; it's so tacky.

"Aye boy! My name is Dani use it!"

I threw my neck back like I was taking Tylenol. They dared me to down the other, no problem. I see Mrs. Cheryl outside smoking the last of a Newport.

The chanting stops when she walks in to the establishment. The waitress escorts her over. Overdressed as usual, in an orchid purple pleated skirt, fully lined jacket to match, complete with silver four inch, open toe Jimmy Choo sandals that wrap around and buckle at her ankles, and sporting a short haircut like Halle Berry, Ms. Thang is fierce. I have to give credit where it is due. With a quick flick of her wrist, her black cat shaped sunglasses were sitting on top of her head.

Watching her sashay to the table I couldn't help but smile. She really got it going on, and I admire her immensely. I document her style in my memory. The way she handles business is like no other. I accompany her in many company meetings. The woman is a tiger when it comes to supply and demand. Crossing every T and doting all Is' commanding respect for her brilliance and knowledge of small business, she is looking to expand the card shop all over the country.

"Hello everyone, I see ya'll starting early," says Mrs. Cheryl

"Why you so late?" Anthony can be irritatingly blunt sometimes.

"Well, if you must know, I just stopped to get Dani's present." She is smiling like she has a secret.

"I heard present, where is it?" I clap my hands to express my joy.

I am always excited when someone gives me something, but I am a terrible gift giver. I never know what to get, and I always tell the surprise. Stephani hates that too.

Inside the small velvet box is a pair of fourteen carat, white gold, diamond stud heart shaped earrings. I couldn't believe it. I rarely wear earrings, but I will be sporting these that's for damn sure! I gave Mrs. Cheryl a hug and ordered another round of shots. We made sure the boss drank as much as everyone else. She was game and had no problem shooting the shots.

Drinking is something the boss lady knows all about. She tells me her habit developed early in life, at age sixteen. This is how she copes with the demons of her past and present. She drinks at work thinking we don't know so we pretend we don't.

"Let me make a toast," Mrs. Cheryl lifts her glass. Her speech is slurred already from two shots. This means she started drinking before she joined the staff party.

"To my protégé, take the bull by the horns and ride! You take all I've taught you and all you've have learned and make the best of it. Keep your head up. I know you can do it."

"Cheers!"

The party is breaking up. We box up all the leftover food and head for the parking area. I sense something strange is about to happen.

"Aye girl, you still gotta let me take you out. This right here doesn't count." Anthony is hollering at me from his car window.

Besides Anthony's good looks, he also dresses nice, always smells like Giorgio Armani, and he knows I love that cologne. If he wasn't trying so hard to be a ladies man, he would be okay. It's his eyes. They are the lightest brown. That's all we hear at the store from the women patrons, "His eyes are gorgeous!" Or "What color are your eyes?" That sets the tone for him then he's in for the kill. It doesn't help with his smooth, deep coffee complexion with a trimmed, coal black goatee and sideburns match his buzz cut precisely. We as women are powerless against a fine ass man.

"Don't worry bout me. You just go home to yo mother." I like to get under his skin as well.

"Oh, so you gon play me like dat in front of your friend…What kinda shit is that?"

"My friend and I are going out. See you when I look atcha, peace." I gave him the peace sign.

We can hear Anthony's music from the other side of the parking lot. Let's Chill by Guy is bumping through the massive speakers. I wonder if he was listening to that before he came in the restaurant or is it for my benefit. I'm certain it is for me. He peels around the parking lot and drives up next to me and Sakoya. Anthony leans out the window, looks directly at me, "Aye for real, I need to have a meetin' with yo body."

He switches the toothpick from one corner of his mouth to the other, using and showing his tongue. I can still smell him.

"What…Why?"

"'Cause yo mind doesn't understand what yo body needs! Holla at me!" He peels out again leaving a cloud of smoke.

We walk over to Sakoya's car to finalize all the details for the night's events. Mrs. Cheryl is parked across from her.

"Now, I see why you didn't want me to talk to him. You want him for yourself." Sakoya's lips are stuck out.

"Girl ple…"

"Don't worry I ain't mad at you. He's fun to be around, he got a job, and he's fine. What color is his eyes?"

I didn't know if I should start explaining myself, because as soon as I start talking, she cuts me off. I love her to death but she has no manners. I try and explain my problem with Anthony and why I don't want him.

"He is twenty five years old…"

"And…" Sakoya's jingling her keys looking at me all crazy.

"Let me finish…Works in a card shop as security! That ain't no job plus he lives at home with his mama. This is what I'm talking 'bout!"

"Oh, excuse me boo boo. Don't you work at that same store?" Sakoya is quick witted also.

"Just shut up and tell me where we going." I don't have the energy to argue with her.

Mrs. Cheryl over hears our conversation.

Miss Kim

"What happened to Frederick?" My very drunk boss yells across the parking lot while unlocking the door of her pearl white Lexus LX 08. It is spotless, as if, it just rolled off the showroom floor. The license plate read, "U C ME."

It's embarrassing enough that he was a no show at my little gathering. He did tell me he had studying to do at the last minute, after I told everybody he was coming. His name is Frederick St. James. I have loved him since we were ten years old. We attended the same elementary and high school. After we graduated, he went off to Florida A & M, and I joined the Air Force. We kept in touch all the while living miles apart. I still have the letters he wrote in a shoe box in the back of my closet. I take them out every now and then just to reminisce and smell them. He would always spray his letters with Drakkar. We made a pact, if we weren't married or engaged by the time we came back home, he and I would marry. Well, we are back, and I am ready to settle down with him; our kids and our picket fence.

"He's over to Pastor's house studying for his exam," I yell back at the boss while still with Sakoya.

"Do you really think that man is going to marry you with all the club hopping and drinking you do? He's not going to marry you! You don't know what you want!"

Mrs. Cheryl is a mean drunk. Wreaks havoc on people then has no recollection the next day.

"Girl, that's your drunk ass boss! Make sure she gets home, and I'll meet you at the club. You know I got to change clothes, and get some candy anyway, but don't take your time!"

I wait until Sakoya drives off. Reluctantly, I sit in the passenger seat of Mrs. Cheryl's car. It wasn't the first time I'd seen the leather trim seats with medium brown walnut wood accents. Even though she's had it awhile, it still has the new car smell. I dream about having a car like this especially with the navigation feature. I am not gifted in the area of directions. I get lost every time. My strange feeling is intensifying.

"Why are you going out with her? Why can't you just stay in with me?" Mrs. Cheryl's tone has changed.

"I was with you all day yesterday and the day before. Damn what do you want?"

I knew exactly what she wanted. Anthony is right; we are more than friends and co workers. I never intended for this to go on for so long, now I regret letting her touch me and vise versa. What started as sexual curiosity now has escalated into a full blown toxic secret relationship.

"We went shopping, remember? I bought all the clothes you have on now, plus the earrings I just gave you. You unappreciative bitch!" She likes to recount all the things she's done for me.

"See, this is what the fuck I'm talking 'bout. Did I ask for this? You can have it all back. I don't give a damn! You bought it 'cause you want to control me, trick no good. You just hoping and wishing I let you do it again, play with it, lick it, and make me shiver, ain't that right? You feel powerful huh? Walking around like you got it like that. You fooled the others, but I run this! You know why I run it? Because I know how bad you want me."

I'm all in her face talking shit. Our lips were inches away from each other. She wants to kiss me, but I slide back in the passenger's seat. For one, we in the damn parking lot of Applebee's and two her breath stinks like day old cigarettes mixed with Vienna sausage juice. Honestly, I like to tease and make her beg. That turned me on just knowing that she would do anything to taste my sweetness. She had nothing to say just looking at me like she wanted me right then and there. I could tell she was getting all flustered in that hot ass suit. It's eighty five degrees in July and she got a fucking suit on trying to impress. Yeah, she's a tiger in those boardroom meetings, but nothing but a twat eatin' cat, when it comes to me.

"Dani please stay just one more night. I promise I won't ask you again. It's just…"

"Just what? Say it. Spit it out!" She is on my last nerve now.

"I dream about you. I really don't know why. I have never felt this way before about any man, and this is the first experience I've ever had with a woman. The way you kiss me, when you look at me, even if you are not around, my thoughts trigger a strong pulsating urge…"

I'm thinking she's about to cry. It's the alcohol making her so emotional, sounding like a soap opera monologue.

"To do what? Girl please. Hate to tell you but that ship has sailed. It was fun while it lasted but it's over and it's time you accept that. I know you want me. If I were you, I'd want me too but get over it! F.Y.I don't ever call me a bitch again. Now run along to your loveless marriage I got some partying to do."

I got out of her car and did my own sashaying to my 2000 flaming red Dodge Neon with tinted windows and matching red masking tape for my busted break light.

Before going out with Sakoya, I stopped over my sister's house to check on her and my two year old daughter, Manasha. I have my own set of keys so I let myself in.

"Hello, hello, hello is anybody home? Where is my precious princess?"

While in the Air Force, I had a relationship with one of the officers on post. We dated for about two and a half years. We had a great time together, but he was being deployed to Japan. He asked me to marry him so we could stay together, but I declined his offer. I loved him but not enough to marry him. After four years, I grew tired of the military life, shuffling around every two years, early morning PT, saluting all the time, etc. Half the time I didn't know who to salute. I just wanted to come home.

The day he left, is the day I found out I was pregnant. I never told him. To this day, he has no idea he has a daughter. She looks just like him, with almond shaped eyes, a cute little pug nose, the complexion of deep chocolate, and a full head of thick coarse auburn hair, that kept me up with heartburn my entire pregnancy. Everyone asks me where did she get that color hair from? I just tell'em our ancestors 'cause I don't know. I'm hoping when she gets older she will start to look more like me. Don't get it twisted ol' boy was fine with a nice grade of hair.

"Hey sweetness," scooping my baby up.

"You ready for your bedtime story? Where's your auntie Stevie?" Mansha couldn't pronounce Stephani.

"No, I don't wanna go." She always looks at me with her little cute eyes when she wants her way.

"How about I read you a story before you go to bed?" We both laugh when I tickle her tummy. Manasha finds her favorite book and climbs into bed.

"Once upon a time, there was a princess named..." I always pause and look at her for the answer.

"'Nassa," the toddler adds. I know she's exhausted. She tries to fight, but loses the battle. I tuck my beautiful baby in and gave her a gentle kiss on the forehead.

"Mommy can I have some water?"

"No 'Nasha I thought you were asleep?"

"Nope. I want some water."

"No, you don't need any water. You will wet the bed. Now close your eyes and go to sleep."

"Well, can I have Mr. Pickles?" Manasha is tryin' me tonight.

Mr. Pickles is the stuffed animal she slept with every night. I can see she is not trying to sleep. When Stephani appears in the door way, Manasha jumps up and runs to her giving her the little cute eyes.

"I don't wanna go…please aunt Stevie tell her not to make me go."

The little girl is a con artist too just like her father!

"Awwwwe! Let her stay up. It's Friday. She can sleep in tomorrow, deal? Plus I want to show you what I added to the nursery?" Stephani is anxious to show me the new room but I'm not through fussing.

"You gon have to stop undermining me. When I say something, I mean it."

"I know. I won't do it again, but did you see those eyes?" Stephani is a push over.

"See that's what I'm talkin' bout. You get mushy around her and she uses you. Then she uses you against me, and I ain't having that. She is spoiled rotten by you." I'm upset with my sister, a little.

It is easy for my daughter to manipulate Stephani because all she wants and thinks about is a child of her own.

"Ta da! What do you think?" Her grin is bright, as if she is going into the delivery room tonight. Walking in the nursery, my mind says this is wrong, but like she says there's nothing wrong with being prepared. Prepared is not the word I would use in describing this room. Picturesque is more like it, but what is disturbing is this room is specifically for a girl child. Stephani has chosen the sex of her imaginary baby.

"It's beautiful sis. It really is." I gave my sister a hug.

I didn't have the heart to talk sensible. Truth is, it's unhealthy for her to direct all her attention on something that may not occur for a while. The way her husband talks it's as if he doesn't want children at all.

"Sis I gotta go. It's lovely. Please don't buy anything else. It's perfect."

"So, where you going anyway?" Stephani wants to spend more time in the nursery.

"Sakoya and I are going out to get our groove on. Something you need to do instead of sitting here everyday babysitting and decorating."

"Well, I'm always babysitting 'cause you always out getting your groove on."

"Oh don't blame that on me. You choose to stay in this big ol' house. I ask you to come with me all the time. Where is Brandon?"

"Please don't start on my husband. I don't need to hear nothing you got say about him. He's at work and at least I got a man!" Stephani is in defense mode.

I hate it when she says *my husband* like he's something. He ain't shit. She likes to throw it in my face that she's married, living the American dream, in her prestigious and spacious, two level, four thousand square foot home, with five bedrooms, four and half bathrooms, a gourmet kitchen with stainless steel appliances, and a breakfast nook. The deck overlooks the woods, and the master bedroom has a Jacuzzi tub and fireplace. On top of all that Stephani doesn't work and they have a maid, Constance. She does all the household duties and lives in the guest house behind their home.

"That maybe so, but you got cobwebs between your legs! When was the last time *your husband* fucked the dog shit out of you?"

"Shut up tramp! Get out of here and get your so called groove on."

"Bye! We still on for tomorrow?"

"Heck yeah, you know I love to beat that ass." She is talking loudly while walking toward the front door.

"Stephani please, you don't even sound right talkin' smack. That's why I'm gon smack you back into reality."

"We will see young grasshopper," Stephani disappears in the house.

I left my phone charging in the car; missed five calls and a text. Right off I know at least three of them are from Mrs. Cheryl. I will check her voice messages later. I know they all say the same thing. As much as I admire her for business savvy and how she manages the store, she sucks when it comes to her self-esteem. I feel bad for the way I treated her earlier, but it seems she just ain't getting' it. Does she really think just because we've had some heated sexual encounters, that I've given up on men? That I don't enjoy a strong man pencil hitting every one of my spots or the aroma of sweat and musk when he comes home from a hard days work? She thinks I'm going to trade the way my stomach jumps at the sight of a tall, beefy, ebony man with chiseled features for a woman with a turkeybaster. Or how I need tissue for my panties just from the sound of his voice? If so, she can kick rocks because I'm just having fun before I tie the knot. I ain't serious about none of it. I'm going to marry Frederick St. James and live happily ever after. It's destiny.

My text is from Frederick instantly my stomach flutters. I hope I can see him tonight. It reads, *"I'm sorry I couldn't make it to ur celebration. Hope u had a good time. Still at Pastor's house. Will call 2mrrw."*

I call Sakoya back.

"What's up, you rang?"

"What up wit you? Why you sounding all dry like that? You don't want to go do you? That's okay. I'll call my other friend. She just broke up with her boyfriend, and she wanted to go out with us. I know how you really don't like her so it's cool."

"Alright, I'll talk to you tomorrow. I got another call coming in."

"Bye girl," Sakoya hangs up.

"Hello?"

"Aye what's up queen? Just calling to see what you're up to." A familiar voice is on the other end.

"Nothin. 'Bout to go home."

"Okay, good. I want you to do something for me. Can you come over for a minute?"

"Like what? You know I don't like you like that," I'm suspicious; he could be talking about anything.

"Just c'mon. I'll be waiting to let you in."

Might as well go. Frederick is studying, and I really don't feel like going home. I can't believe I'm going over there again. I wonder what he wants me to do this time?

Miss Kim

/enjoy running in the mornings especially on Saturday. I get a lot of thinking done. My mind wonders about the neighbors working in their yards. Wondering what kind of people are they? What problems they have.

This morning my thoughts replay all the events of yesterday starting with Mrs. Cheryl. I know we've messed up our friendship because nothing has been the same since we had our encounters. I had no idea this is such a big deal to her because she's married. I know they have their problems, but don't all married couples have problems? I was under the impression she could handle our special relationship but it appears she wants more. I'm sorry, but I have no more to give.

This observation brings me to Frederick. I'm willing to do anything for him, for us. He is the one for me. I've always known that. We have the same ambition; want the same things out of life. Right now, he's extremely busy working towards our future. When will he make time for us?

After my run and exhilarating shower, I feel great knowing in a couple of hours I will have to deal with my boss. Usually, I work for my father at his hardware store every Saturday. I promised him we would do our inventory next week. Today I'm going in early to record the supply at the card shop. I asked for the extra hours to learn how Mrs. Cheryl does it. Every time the auditor comes to check on things we always get the thumbs up first time through, that's rare. I will take that knowledge and help my father with his.

I arrive at the job on time. I say a little prayer before going in, "Dear Lord, please let there be peace and harmony today. Please forgive me for the way I've acted towards my boss in Jesus name I pray, amen."

I take a deep breath, clock in, and put my purse away. Boss lady is in her office. I hesitate before going in.

"Good Morning Mrs. Cheryl. How are you today?"

"Good morning, we need to get a head start before the others come in. Here is a marker and clipboard. I've already sectioned off the area you will cover. Use the marker only if the count on the paper doesn't match what's actually on the shelves. I started last night, so there is only a few more to do."

Mrs. Cheryl is strictly business this morning. No sign of the weakling I left in the car last night, what a relief. When she shows me the area I have to count, I realize the weakling is hiding behind this façade. The area is humungous and needs to be counted before I leave for the day. I clocked in two hours early; clearly I need more time to make sure it is correct. I know she did this on purpose. That's okay. I will handle it, but she's a butthole. When she asked me to do this, it was my understanding that we would do it together. After showing the area to me, she retreats to her office. Instead of complaining, which is what she wants me to do, I smile and start counting.

Before I knew it, the other employees were clocking in. I wasn't close to being done. Mrs. B. shows up first.

"Good morning Mrs. B. How are you doing?" I ask.

"Alright I guess, ol' Arthur trying to act up on me that's about it. How you?

"Just trying to count this crap."

Miss Kim

"I'm glad it's you and not me. Let me get ready. Oh, how was the party yesterday?"

"It was wonderful. I'm sorry you couldn't make it."

"I was at prayer meeting. You coming to church Sunday?"

"Yes ma'am."

Mrs. B., is the cashier, her drawer never comes up short even if "Arthur" acts up, her nickname for Arthritis. Sometimes it slowed her down, but she kept on going and never complained.

"Hi Dani! I forgot you were coming in early. How was the rest of the party?" Nadine whizzes by to get in the empty bathroom.

"I'll tell you all about it later." Mrs. Cheryl is looking at me through the windows. That meant get back to work.

Mrs. Cheryl hired Nadine a week before me, and we work great together. I consider her one of my closest and dearest friends. She lives vicariously through me and my escapades (except the one with the boss). She loves working at the store and listening to my wild stories. It is an escape from her life, one filled with drinking and abuse.

She confides in me, tales I've only seen on the lifetime channel. I can only imagine what she goes through on a daily basis. Stewart started drinking when she told him she was pregnant again. He became abusive to her and the boys after a night of drinking at the local tavern, but she still loves him. "It's just a phase" is her reasoning for his behavior. He asked Nadine to get an abortion, but she refused.

Because of the torment, she is absent frequently, was even hospitalized a few times. I leave the room when she tells her stories of why she's late or didn't get to work. She thinks we don't know Stewart beats her, so we pretend we don't. I hate seeing her in so much pain. She and I visit women shelters, we called the anonymous hotline for battered women once, but she hung up before someone answered. She has pamphlets and all types of information on abuse, nothing works.

Anthony is the last person to clock in. He strides in the office to get the first doughnut, it's a ritual, "Good morning to you to Miss Lady. Aye, when you gon let me take you out?"

"I'm not! I don't date men I work with, and you can't afford me anyway!" My neck is in motion.

"Baby, you know I gots plenty of money," flashing his stack of ones, grinnin' hard with the glistening gold pullout tooth showing.

We both laugh. I couldn't help it. This man really thinks he is God's gift to all women; always in the clubs trying to take someone home, to *their* home that is. He claims he lives at home so he can save money. The rest of his money is spent on clothes, and expensive accessories for his car. He spends a lot of time restoring his 1969 Chevy Mustang. His exact words to me were: "I will never grow up."

Over lunch one day, I learned a few things about the Romeo of security. He graduated from Ohio State University with a Bachelors degree of Fine Art. He was a part of a development team to put various art projects in our downtown area.

We are all amazed at the signs and tags he draws on the display windows. He says it's just a hobby and nothing more. I try to explain to him that he is letting the talent the Lord gave him go to waste. All he is interested in is money, weed, and women, in that order. He said he will concentrate on the "art thang" when the time is right.

"The time is now," I let him know.

"Yeah, yeah, yeah whatever. all I want to know is when can I take you out?" Lunch is over for me.

Boss lady checks the front of the store to make sure everything is running smoothly. She comes back to my inventory section where I am counting and documenting many cards, envelopes, etc. She asks to see what I have accomplished so far. I feel I've had done quite a bit, but I guess I ain't moving fast enough. She grabs a red pen from her jacket to correct any and all mistakes I'm making.

"Listen, I want to apologize to you for yesterday. I may have overreacted a little."

Mrs. Cheryl keeps her back to me the entire time paying close attention to the inventory task at hand. She nods letting me know she heard the apology. That kinda pisses me off because I'm trying to express myself and all I get is a nod, whatever. We work in silence.

She broke the deafening silence by explaining the mistakes. I listen intently not interrupting her explanation. I can tell she is uneasy around me, good. I did my part. The ball is in her court now.

"It's very important that you keep an accurate account of the stock coming in and the merchandise you sell. Precise recordkeeping is key in running a successful business. You will need this information when opening your own store. That's the plan right?"

"Yes that's plan," I'm caught off guard

when she asks the question.

"Youre gonna leave me and become my competition?"

"I'm afraid so… Don't think of it like that. Think of it as one of your finest pupils making her way, and I do mean finest. God will make room for both our thriving businesses."

I am relieved when she chuckles at my little joke. She is receptive to the hug I give her. I continue my long, boring job for the day while she checks the front again.

She returns in better spirits ready to help me with the daunting task. Now breezing through inventory Mrs. Cheryl began to open up about her personal life.

She starts telling me about her fifteen year old son, Jeremiah. He lives in Colorado with his father. I'm surprised at his age. This meant she was sixteen when he was born. She dropped out of school to take care of her son. Being a young mother proved to be very difficult, so she gave Jeremiah to his father who was much older and stable.

This turn of events, changed her life forever. She vowed to get her GED and make something of herself. I can see why she is so driven. Mrs. Cheryl has never seen her son in person only in pictures. She sends money, clothes, and the latest videogames, whatever he needs.

"Why haven't you seen him?"

"His father has since married, and they have a child together. I don't want to disrupt their home or Jeremiah's life. He is stable and happy. That's all I want for him is to be happy. Maybe one day he will forgive me," She is on the verge of tears.

I explain to her, "Every child needs to know

their birth parents. They need an explanation of why things happened the way they did. It is their right to know the truth, you owe him that. Jeremiah needs to know you and his family. You don't have to take him away from his father to do that. It will not ruin his life. It will enhance his quality of life knowing his birth mother truly does love him, and you did what was best for him. It may be hard at first but it will all work out. First, you need to forgive yourself."

I rubbed my boss' shoulders and left her with her thoughts. As I walk toward the front of the store I say a silent, "thank you Jesus". Prayer really does work. I thought my day would be horrible because of yesterday but it is just the opposite. God even gave me the comforting words for a mother longing for her son's forgiveness. It always makes me feel good and grateful for my life because it could be worse. If only I can do the same for Nadine before it's too late.

The workday went fast since I was in the back all day counting. On my way home, I concocted my strategy for tonight. I haven't seen or talked to Frederick so I hope to see him tonight.

Before our little rendezvous, I have to school my big sister on the art of shooting pool. We shoot every Friday night in her game room. Manasha is already over there, but I need her to stay until tomorrow, so I can spend some quality time with Frederick. Here I am making these plans, and I don't even know for sure if I'm going to see him.

In my small apartment, I put the plan in motion first then I call Stephani.

"Hey sis, I just got off work. You want me to come and get 'Nasha?" I ask her this in hopes that she will say "no". If she says "yes", I've got to pull a trick move on her. I know I should be ashamed but I'm not.

"I thought we discussed us shooting tonight because of your little party, plus it's the tiebreaker anyway."

"Oh yeah, I forgot. I am just trying to give you a break. Let me get ready, and I'll be there to spank that ass. You not going anywhere are you?" This question is just to make sure she doesn't have any plans for after the match.

"No, I'll be here."

I jump in the shower, put on my Red Door body lotion with perfume, and a comfortable short set. I make another phone call.

"Hello, I'm sorry I'm not here to take your call. If you would please leave your name, number and a brief message I will return your call immediately," says the voicemail.

"Hi there, you know who this is, I'm going to have some free time tonight (assuming my sister will keep my daughter). I thought we could get together if you're not too busy. Call me either way. I'll be waiting."

I grab my custom made, engraved pool stick and case, given to me as a Christmas gift from my dear sister last year and a little bag then out the door I went.

Arriving at my sister's house twenty minutes later, I knock on Menasha's door and a little voice yells.

"Who is dis?"

"It's your mommy," I hear my little two year old screaming, "Mommy, mommy, it's mommy!"

The door opens; she jumps into my arms and

gives me a big hug. One of the most gratifying feelings is my child's little arms around my neck.

"What have you been doing sweetness? Mommy missed you today. Have you been good?" Manasha nods "yes" and out of my arms into the kitchen. She comes back with a new stuffed bear in her hands. I bend down to get a closer look.

"Nook mommy, see what I got?" She presses the bear right in my face.

"Who bought you that?"

"Auntie Stevie," the baby announces.

I know she spends too much time over here, but it is so much cheaper than a daycare or babysitter. Our parents keep her sometime but they have busy schedules too. I'm really scared to leave her with someone I'm not familiar with. I don't trust people like that with my baby; most mothers prefer someone they know.

I depend on my sister a great deal. That's what older siblings are here for right? Stephani would not allow me to take her anywhere else. Sometime I worry about my sister. Is this healthy for her?

"You ready for your whippin' little girl," Stephani is rubbing her hands together like a wicked witch. She's so corny.

"Whatever oldylock. Fix my drink. As I recall, it's one and one. You claim you were too tired to finish last week."

"Just rack'em!" Stephani ordered while she made the drinks.

The game is underway when Stephani's husband, Brandon breezes in, then right back out.

I am lining up for my next shot, but all I can think about is Brandon not even giving his wife a kiss, not letting her know where he is going. I know it's not my business but damn.

"Does he ever pay attention to you?"

"Don't start. We are having a good time, please." Stephani took a long sip of her potent drink.

I sank the high ball and decided to leave it alone. I'm walking around the table to find the best shot and out of nowhere it comes out.

"He is a good provider. I'm sure you can see that. Just look around! You are standing on tempting red elegant swirl Stainmaster carpet. He loves me! You are just jealous because you don't have a man! So you can't tell me shit about a man!"

"See this is what I'm talkin' about! I haven't said anything else but there you go runnin' off at the mouth! I don't want a man, especially if he treats me like that bastard treats you! I'm too young and fine to let one man tie me down, and I do mean fine, thank you very much." I stopped in front of one of the many mirrors in the room to check my face and hair.

"You ain't nothin but a tramp. When are you going to settle down and find a father for your baby? That's what you need to do," Stephani is lining up her second shot.

"Don't you worry about me and my status. You keep concentrating on you and yours. I see you like calling me a tramp. I'll let you get that one off, but at least I'm getting' some, *virgin!*"

Stephani laughs and still sinks the eight ball.

"Rack'em!" She yells. I can tell she's feeling good. She is not a drinker so one does her swell. My sister and I have this argument all the time. We never let our disagreements go to far but we do say what we mean. I try not to be too harsh, I

know I could grill her if I want to but choose not to.
I rather make her laugh. I love her too much, and
she does so much for me that I couldn't hurt her.

Stephani has finished her first drink and now
is making a second. I go over to check my cell
phone in my purse. I have a missed a call.

"Hey Stephani, I'm going to go and check
on Nasha, okay? I'll be right back. Sit down and
drink that so you don't spill it on your *Stainmaster
carpet*." I brought my phone with me so I can
check the message.

I went into Nasha's room. She is sleeping
on top of her Dora the Explorer table, with Lilo and
Stitch playing on her DVD player. There is a strong
odor in her room, not a bad odor, but something. I
put the phone down to check around to see what the
mischievous little girl has been into. I see nothing
at first glance, as I lift Nasha off the table and into
the bed. I smell the odor strongly. It is apparent that
she has some kind of perfume on. After removing
the pink feather boa from around her neck and
matching pink slippers off her feet to tuck her in, I
check her dressing mirror (a replica of Stephani's
dressing mirror complete with lights). There it is an
empty bottle of Daisy Duck perfume by Disney. I
laugh. She is a little princess to her core. I
remembered buying her this particular bottle. She
didn't want the Bubbles Power Puff perfume by
Cartoon Network because it didn't look expensive
like Stephani's.

I close the door and return to my business. I
call Frederick back.

"Hello?"

"Hey, how are you doing? I'm really sorry
about Friday. You know I'm studying to pass this
test. I heard your message. I'm free tonight if you

want to get together."

That is all I need to hear, "Yeah sure, I want to get together. Let me clear the rest of my schedule, and I'll call you back."

"Oh, okay. Talk to you soon then."

"Bye."

I couldn't let him know I'm sitting here waiting on him to call. Well, my plan is working so far. Now, I have to go and check on my sister and see where her head is, swimming in Vodka I hope.

"Well, I guess you can be queen for a weekend, but you won't be so lucky next week." I'm walking into the game room where Stephani has fallen asleep in Brandon's lounge chair.

"Stephani...Stephani...I am tugging at her sweatpants. Hey, I'm going to go ahead and go. You better get up to bed. Nasha is already asleep, and I don't want to wake her up."

"You better not wake her up! She's fine here with me. I got her."

"I know you do."

"But she doesn't have her Sunday clothes here."

We turn everything off. I unscrewed my pool stick and return it to its case. Brought the glasses upstairs. Stephani walks me to the door. She is a little more coherent.

"You going to church in the morning aren't you?"

"Yeah, why?"

"You gon come all the way out here to bring Nasha's clothes?"

"Oh yeah, hold on. Stay right here for a minute," I left with my stick and purse towards my car.

I put my things down and grab the things in

the little bag from the backseat and went back to the door.

"What did you forget?"

Holding a little yellow lace dress, slip, stockings and white patented leather shoes, I announce, "Here's Nasha's church clothes. They just happen to be in my backseat. Can you believe that?" I am smiling so hard it makes Stephani laugh.

"You bitch," She snatches the clothes from me.

"Don't forget her purse. The hair bows and barrettes are inside." Stephani snatches that too. I back away and blow goodbye kisses to my big sister. She closes the door in my face. I pulled my cell phone out, "I'm on my way."

I park my car across the street from Frederick's apartment. I check myself in the mirror, pop in a peppermint with two quick strokes of my Cover girl Outlast Sparkling Wine lip color, and I'm ready. On my way up to the porch, my feelings are running rampant. I start to feel dizzy like I was in high school going over a boy's house when his parents weren't home. Deep down, I know I shouldn't be doing this, but I can't help it. I want to go and test the forbidden waters.

That's what it is; I want what I can't or shouldn't have. I ask myself why? Why can't I have it? I want it so I should have it. When I get it because I always get it, I have to keep it quiet, secret. I love secrets. You will find no one that hasn't had a secret, told a secret or heard a secret. They have their own entrance into a conversation, "Don't tell nobody but..." Their own exit, "You didn't hear nothing from me."

Even better than having or knowing a secret

is creating one. The fact of knowing something only I and another person knows is exciting and very much dangerous.

I gained control over my nervousness. Before I knock, the door opens.

"Hi, what took you so long, and what's that behind your back?" His smile is bright accentuating his dimples.

"Can I get in the door first before you interrogate me?"

Slowly moving my left hand from around my back, I watch the expression on his face.

"Oh wow, this is thoughtful!" He gives me the biggest hug and kiss on the cheek, "Thank you baby, no one has ever given me a rose before," I like when he calls me baby, "Have a seat while I go put this in some water."

I watch Frederick disappear into the kitchen. Pure by saxophonist Boney James is playing softly in the background. His apartment was dimly lit with several candles burning, giving off a masculine, but appealing scent.

I have longed for this man since I was ten! I met him in the fifth grade. He would sit across from me in lunch but never really talk to me; he was always reading. We didn't start talking to each other until the next year. We had English Literature, and wood shop classes together. Our connection had been strictly platonic, except the time in his mother's basement when we were fifteen years old. My stomach still jumps when I think of how he pressed me against the wall with his body. He looked directly into my eyes, I could feel his breath on my face. He said to me, "I want to kiss you."

We started a fire between us that night that

has never burned out. Frederick forever the gentleman rarely pressed the issue of sex because he respected me. He figured if it was meant to happen it would without us trying to make it happen.

Nonetheless, the chemistry is still there; explosive chemistry. After all this time we have never acted on our feelings for fear that it could do more harm than good. Frederick has stated his main focus is to finish school. Everything else would have to wait. We began going out on little dates about four months ago. Each date is more intense then the last. Maybe tonight will prove to be the night we've dreamt of since the basement.

"What's been up? Keeping out of trouble I hope," Frederick asks as he put his arm around me moving in close.

"I'm good. Just came from my sisters house."

"How is Stephani doing?"

"Fine, I guess."

"Is everything OK?"

"Yeah, she just wants a baby so bad. I hope she doesn't fall into a deep depression about it. Her husband is such a jerk! He knows she wants a baby, and he keeps putting her off. It's not fair."

"Well, maybe he is not ready to have a baby just yet."

"I think it's more than that. I think he is having an affair."

"You cannot go around accusing this man for something you have no proof of."

"I know he will cheat because he came on to me."

"When?"

"He and my sister were arguing one night while I was over there. The argument started before

I got there and had escalated. They decided to stop fighting until I left. My sister and I were shooting pool, like always, and she went to the store for some ice. While she was gone, he came into the poolroom and started talking to me about their problems. It was cool until he tried to kiss me. Telling me he wished he'd married me instead of Stephani. Then he was trying to touch me, and I pushed him away. I told him to never come near me, and if he did, I would tell Stephani."

"So you have never told your sister about this?"

"No. She would think I was lying, and I know how much she loves him. I wouldn't want to hurt her. Besides, nothing happened."

"I don't know what to tell you. Maybe that was the right thing. If he is having an affair, the truth will come out."

This is why I like Frederick. He can hold a conversation that doesn't revolve around him and all he's accomplished. He is a great listener, advice giver, and I am confident all his dreams will come true. Every time he opens his mouth, I get turned on.

"What you lookin' at?" Realizing I'm not paying attention but looking straight at his mouth.

"I'm watching your lips move."

He doesn't know whether to keep talking or to stop. He starts again. I move closer to his face.

"Go on, continue talking," I whisper directly to his face.

"It's kinda hard with your face so close to mine," Frederick whispers in my ear.

"What's hard?"

I know I'm making him a little uncomfortable, but he is not shying away. My body is feeling warmer. I want him to touch me all over, fill a desire that arouses me in my dreams; A fever only he can control.

"Would you like for me to move?"

"No," Frederick is still whispering.

I kiss Frederick softly. I lick his lips slowly opening his mouth inviting my tongue in. I watch him close his eyes. Our breathing is deep as we explore each other's mouths. He handles me like fine China ready to be mounted on a sturdy perch. The passion is sweet and sticky like honey between my fingers. I kiss his neck and suck on his earlobe. He runs his hand through my hair pulling it slightly. My hands stroking his body sent warm sensations through me. I want him now, right now.

Frederick enjoys every kiss and caress. His breath is hot in my ear. It makes me moist deep between my thighs. I delve into his mouth again with unrelenting fervor. I can hear deep moans as he returns my kisses with just as much eagerness.

Looking deep into his brown eyes, unbuttoning his shirt revealing his well-sculptured chest, I run my hands softly over the rippling muscles. Discovering his powerful nakedness sends me into a whirlwind of passion. I take his shirt off slowly kissing every inch of his torso. Frederick lies his head back to enjoy my display of affection.

Unbuttoning my blouse, he is not prepared for the "girls." Adorning them is an embroidered hunter green, satin lace plus bra, my favorite from Hips and Curves, I unbutton it and let it fall to the floor. I feel the bulge through his jeans. He straddles me taking my whole essence in. He releases some throbbing pressure by unzipping his jeans revealing the top of his red bikini underwear. Sliding his upper body against mine, I felt like I was right back in that basement. His hands explore my body carefully kissing my neck. I moan with anticipation. He plants sweet, fiery kisses all over my aching flesh. He takes my breast in his mouth sucking feverishly first the left, then the right, running his tongue around and around. I arch my back and ran my hands through his hair as he teases me with his exploring tongue.

The fragrance emanating from his body mesmerizes me. His skin tastes like sweet berries, ripe with richness. His aura envelopes me like a warm, thick blanket on cold winter nights. He wants me, and he can't hold back any longer, kissing my navel playfully watching my body writhe with pleasure. He massages my well toned legs and strong inner thighs. I spread them slowly enticing him in.

I want to rip off all my clothes, but I take a deep breath and relax. Frederick stops for a moment to make sure I want to continue. He whispers, "Do you want me?"

I respond with a passionate kiss and a definite "Yes." He's unbuttoning my shorts as the butterflies dance in my stomach. Under my shorts were my matching v-cut, satin hunter green panties.

He takes off all my clothes then I watch him undress. Men don't think we enjoy watching them taking their clothes off, lordy we do. Admiring their physique, appreciating their manhood, and making them feel like no other. He is a debonair prince ready to take his princess to her dreams where he is the leading man. An overflowing passion fills me. My dreams are unfolding right before my eyes.

We lay naked on the floor deciding to move to his bed where it's more comfortable. Our bodies move in unison to the hypnotic music of moans, groans, and kissing deep. He starts rubbing my thigh; it is warm. I feel his fingers explore my inner most succulent sanctum causing my legs to spread; it is hot. I plunged my tongue deeper in his mouth as the warm fingers rub my special button.

"Oooooh, it feels so good. Don't stop."

"Never," he whispers.

Frederick shows me what he's made of, parting my legs, and French kissing my special button over and over. Oh my Gooodnessss!

"Ohhh my gooodnesss! Ooohh myyy gooodnesssss! OOOOhhhh right there! Right there!" I let him know that tongue is hitting that special button just right!

He is relentless making me feel it…Making my body shake like a thunderous volcanic eruption. He could hear my loud declaration of satisfaction, see my heavenly expression, and taste my juicy bliss. "OOOOhhhhh Frrreeedddyyyy!"

"You like?" He whispers as he comes up for air.

My mind and body is encompassed in sexual rapture at this point, and I'm ready for whatever Frederick has in-store.

He's teasing me with his rock hard man pencil rubbing slowly against me. I open my legs pulling him into me. He looks deep in my eyes while entering my sacred place. The passion and desire is so high in the room; he thrusts deeper.

I felt Frederick's thrusts, but I didn't feel him! I really hate when I get with a dude and he ain't packing! I took a gander at his man pencil. There is no way Frederick could go deep. His manhood lacks manliness.

Nevertheless, he is everything I want in a

man, a father, and a husband. His manly
deficientcy is not enough for me to give up on what
I've wanted since the first day I met him. We share
an intimate rhythmic dance of lovemaking. I move
my body in unison with Frederick creating pulsating
pressure on my button. OOOhhhh, I wanted him
deep but he pulls out his sausage-like unit, rubs it
against my warm, creamy private lips until he
bellows out a loud moan.

As we lay in each other's arms, my love for
him is immense. I didn't want to move. He holds
me close, melting me into his protective arms. My
thoughts are running all over the place as I lay on
his hairy chest. I can't believe it happened or it's
happening. my dreams of being Mrs. Frederick St.
James are slowly coming true.

"Dani, I love being here with you. You have
no idea how much you mean to me. You are a
beautiful woman," He glided his hand through my
freshly permed hair.

I've heard it all before. I just hope he
means me as a person is beautiful not just my sex. I
quickly dismiss this thought from my mind. I know
Frederick is different from all the other guys I've
dated. I know how serious he takes his life and
future. He always keeps it real with me. This is the
beginning of our promising future together.

Miss Kim

/almost overslept reminiscing over every detail of the night before. I am still floating on my love cloud. Although my conscience won't allow me to fully enjoy last night's bliss, because I did have unprotected sex with Frederick. I was so caught up I broke one of my own rules. I only use condoms as my main source of protection to be absolutely certain I'm safe. There are other things out there besides babies. Maybe in my subconscious I know he will be my husband, so it's okay. Should we happen to go down that path again there will be no more mistakes. I don't want any more kids until I'm happily married.

My love cloud began to rain all over my perfect evening with Frederick. I replayed every detail. Frederick did reassure me he did "pull out" before he came. I calm myself, *I'm not pregnant so don't worry about it.*

In all my deep thinking, I hadn't noticed the flashing light on my answering machine. I love the flashing light, it means someone, somewhere is thinking about me. Usually I want to see who's called, but I will wait unit after church to return them. I want to keep this great feeling I have for as long as I can. It doesn't last long because I had to call my sister.

"Hey sis how is everything? Is my baby up and ready to go?"

"Yeah, girl you know we on our way. She looks so precious; she was a good girl all morning."

I could tell Manasha is sitting right there listening to every word "Aunt Stevie" has to say. I can hear her in the background asking to speak to me.

"Hi mommy," the little voice sings.

"Hi shuga-bear."

Her little voice is music to my ears. I can't wait to see what she looks like in her new clothes. Stephani is back on the line.

"We will see you there at the church. Save our seats."

"How many?" I only ask to see if her husband, the jerk, would be there this morning.

"Just two, for me and my 'Nasha," she plays with the toddler over the phone.

"Where is your *husband*?"

Stephani hangs up on me. That's okay I'm still on my cloud partly because I will see the man of my dreams in just a few minutes. I wonder if he is thinking of me and our night. Just in case, I made sure I wore my favorite, a stretch knit jersey dress with a wrap bodice. I love the way I look in this dress. I get compliments every time I wear it. I pin my hair up elongating my neck, so I can wear all of my knock-off accessories. I'm looking in the rear view mirror at myself and not the traffic behind me waiting for me to turn at the green light I didn't see.

Inside the church, I didn't know how to feel or how to act. It is all euphoric for me; all my thoughts are of Frederick No one in the church knows we are seeing each other. We decided to keep things on the hush until we knew for sure. As for me, I'm ready to shout it through the roof top, "I'm in love with Frederick St. James!"

My sister, Manasha, and I are sitting in the same pew we sit in every Sunday enjoying the morning's festivities. I spot Mrs. B. sitting in her usual spot. I blow her a kiss. Our parents have taken their rightful places; mom with the Sunshine Seniors, dad standing down front with the deacons. Mr. Thompson is president of the deacon board and the most handsome.

Manasha was busy looking through her little patent leather purse, taking everything out then putting back in.

I'm looking around for my love slave trying not to be obvious.

"Who you looking for?" Stephani whispers.

"Nobody."

"He isn't in here yet."

"Who are you talking about?"

Stephani looks around herself and finally said, "Him."

A man dressed in a two-button classic black pinstriped suit breezes through the sanctuary doors and takes a seat on the first pew. The sight of him fills my stomach with butterflies again. I cross my legs to calm the wanton desire I feel growing between them.

"I am not looking for him!" Immediately I motion for the usher to bring me a fan.

The entire congregation stands in preparation for the Morning Hymn. The organist plays its introduction and the choir director raises his arms; the congregation sings.

"Blessed Assurance Jesus is mine, Oh what a foretaste of Glory divine..."

Manasha stands on the pew singing as loud as she can. Mumbling words only she understands. She holds the bulletin upside down and copies the churchgoers in front of her. When they clap, she claps. We try our best not to laugh at her antics but it is impossible. Usually Manasha attends the Nurturing Nursery. However, it is the first Sunday of August, and all the children are upstairs in the sanctuary. Manasha is a humble baby, and she usually sits quietly, but the August heat is causing a little stir among all the little ones this particular morning. I keep little things in my purse to keep 'Nasha busy.

After the morning hymn and scripture reading, the choir director seats the congregation. I glance towards the distinguished looking man on the first pew.

"Stop staring at the man and pay attention!" Stephani whispers sternly.

I tried to concentrate on the assisting pastor, Reverend White, as I adjusted in the pew. Manasha has fallen asleep in Stephani's lap with beads of sweat formed around her hairline. A steady flow of air provided by fanning kept her serene.

It's offering time, and I have my tithes ready. I always feel good when I have my ten percent; mama always stresses the importance of tithing. She would say, "Without the Lord and His grace you wouldn't have anything. He is the one who blessed you with what you have today. Ten percent is a small amount to ask. Look what He has done for you and will do for you. When you give, you will receive blessings in return."

My sister and I were active members of the church when we were younger, but somehow we have drifted away from our spiritual work. I feel guilty sometimes just sitting here in the same pew Sunday after Sunday. Although my work in the church has been temporarily disconnected, I know I have a relationship with the Lord. I know, if I don't put Him first in everything, it will fail.

As the tray is being passed, I look over at my Freddie. He's sitting over there looking like my husband. We have waited long enough. It's time we take this to the next level.

"Reverend Booker is suffering from

laryngitis," Rev. White explains the Pastor has been to one of his son's basketball games and was one of the loudest, therefore he wouldn't be preaching today. There is movement in the congregation. Everybody loves Rev. Booker. If he isn't preaching on Sunday, half of the members won't come to service. Rev. White goes on to announce, one of the associate ministers will bring forth the Word.

"This young man has come a long way. We all have known him since he was a youngster singing in the youth choir. I remember when he was about ten years old and gave a riveting performance of Malcolm X in our youth revival. I said to myself, 'this boy is going to make it big.'"

He has completed his four years of college majoring in Theology, on the Dean's List I might add. Now, in his second year of Seminary school, this young man makes me proud. He preached his Trial Sermon here last year, and we were all uplifted and proud to have him as one of our own. Please welcome with me our own Mr. Frederick St. James."

Church service was wonderful and dinner at Red Lobster was filling. My father always takes the whole family out to eat after service, except when he had to count the monies taken in on his appointed Sunday.

Inside my cramped apartment, Manasha is in her room playing with her dolls. Stephani is talking to me while I start the dish water.

"What's wrong?" It seems something is on her mind.

My phone rang. I rush to it like Flo Jo in hopes that it's Freddy on the other end.

"Hey, what's up girl?" Sakoya says.

"I tried to call you yesterday but you weren't in. Did you get my message?"

"No, let…"

"Girl, last night we went to …"

"Sakoya!"

"What?"

"I gotta call you back. I'm in the middle of something."

"I was too until you interrupted me. Dang you are so rude…"

"Bye 'Koya."

I get back to the kitchen, and my sister is putting lipstick on my child.

"Take that off of her. She will have it all over the place! Now, what is wrong with you?"

"Nothing you don't already know."

I can tell by her tone it's about having a baby. Did Mom say something to trigger this episode of unhappiness? It's no surprise. Stephani's been having these moods about a baby for awhile now.

"Maybe ya'll need to see a marriage

counselor or something," I suggested.

"I'm not crazy. I just want to have a baby. Is that too much to ask?"

"Did you hear me? I said ya'll. What's-his-face needs to go too. He does not understand *your* need to have this baby and doesn't seem willing to bend a little. You are not seeing *his* need to be this moneymaking business tycoon, and you don't want to bend a little. You need someone to help you sort through all of this. You can't do it alone."

"I guess you're right," She put the make up back in her purse.

"I'm always right."

"Whatever."

"Are you going to divorce him?" I ask her this to prove my point.

"NO!!"

"Well, you have no other choice. Ask him about it. It will work out fine. Is it on for Friday?"

"Why wouldn't it be? I have to regain my title," Stephani sighs hard as if a weight has been lifted, even if it is only for a moment.

"Whatever, just have the table ready when I get there. Thank you."

I walk Stephani to the door and give her a kiss on the cheek. Stephani smiles and blows Manasha a kiss. Manasha blows one back and says, "Bye Aunt Stevie."

After cleaning the kitchen, I felt like giving the whole apartment a quick once over. On my way to get the vacuum cleaner, the phone rang again. I know it's Sakoya trying to tell me about last night when she went out. I decide against answering because whoever is on the other end will take me out of my cleaning mode, but I will listen to see if they will leave a message. They don't, but I can't resist the flashing light.

The first message is from Mrs. Cheryl.

"Hello Dani, this is Mrs. Cheryl. There's an annual conference for small businesses I attend every year. Atlanta has been chosen to host the conference this year. It's three days and two nights. I thought this would be a great opportunity for you to learn more about opening your own business. The conference isn't until September if you can't make that one there is another in March. The one held in March will be on an Island. Maybe you might want to think about it. We won't be staying in the same room or anything like that. This is strictly business, so you don't have to worry. I will show you the itinerary at work tomorrow. Call me when you get a chance or we can talk at work tomorrow. Bye."

Immediately I think the worst. I know she will do anything to get me alone, especially out of town, but I can't afford not to learn all I can about the business. Next message:

"Dani!… Dani! Are you there? If you are pick up…Girl, I was calling' to see if you wanted to go out to a new club that just opened on the West side called Giorgio's, but since you aren't there, I guess you can't go. I guess I will have to go with JaBrea again. I don't want to go with her though. She makes me sick. She will probably complain all-night and talk about her boring life. Where you at anyway? If I could remember your cell number I would track you down. Oh, I know you are probably with Freddie, huh? Is that it Miss Thang…"

Sakoya's message cut off in mid-sentence. Sakoya uses all the time allotted for her messages. I never understood why she has to talk so much about nothing. Single with no children. I guess she is free to do whatever she wants.

"Um..Hello. Uhh.. This is Mr. Rogers. I am the neighbor of Miss Nadine. She dialed this number and she has…Well my wife and I are going to take her to the hospital. She is in bad shape. If you know Miss Nadine, she will be in St. Mary's Hospital."

"Oh my God! 'Nasha! Nasha! Put your shoes on we gotta go. Hurry baby."

It only takes seven minutes to get to the hospital but it seems like an eternity. On the way in the hospital I pray.

"Please Jesus let her be all right. Keep her surrounded in your love and safe away from harm. I don't know what it is going to take for her to leave that man only you know. Jesus give me the words to say to comfort her, Amen."

We found Nadine's room. There is a young, nice looking police officer standing by. I hesitate before going in.

"Excuse me ma'am, I'm Officer Peterson. I'm sorry to do this but do you know Nadine Hughes very well?"

"Yes, we are friends and coworkers…'Nasha sit down over there please."

"Is there anything you can tell me about what happened last night?"

"No, I wasn't with her last night. I received a call from her neighbor saying she was beaten up pretty bad, and she ran to their house where she passed out. Did you get a chance to talk to them?"

"Yes I did."

"If you don't mind can you tell me what happened to Nadine."

"Well, I don't know much, but I know her boyfriend was taken in last night for disturbing the peace. Another neighbor called in to report loud screaming, doors slamming, and such. When I reached their address, Miss Nadine was gone and Stewart is that his name?"

"Yes"

"He was past out on the floor with door wide open. I couldn't get anything from him because he was too drunk."

"I'm sorry I can't be of more assistance, but I don't know anything." I shrugged my shoulders.

"Thank you for your time. You can go in but I don't suggest your daughter go in with you. I have to stay here for awhile so I can watch her for you."

"Thank you. I won't be long. Manasha I will be right back. Sit here and talk to Officer Peterson but not too much, okay?"

"Okay mommy."

Scared of what my friend looks like, my heart begins to race. I take a deep breath, "Jesus help me," and enter the room.

The shades are closed. Dim lights are on behind her head. The very dull middle curtain is drawn for privacy. Nadine lay motionless in her bed. I walk in slowly, careful not to awaken her. My heart drops when I see the head bandage, swollen eyes, and busted lips, black and blue contusions on her legs and feet. It took all I had not to cry. I can barely recognize my co-worker and friend. Uncontrollable tears race down my cheeks. I place Nadine's hand in mine and begin to pray silently.

"Jesus lay your hands on my friend. Make her well, take special care of her baby," Nadine tries

to grip the hand she's holding, slowly opening her
eye.

"Who's there?" Nadine strains to speak
"It's me, Dani," A lump is in my throat.
"Hey Swee..."
"Your neighbors left a message on my
machine Saturday night. I just got it today. I'm so
sorry I wasn't here for you when you needed me. Is
the baby all right?" I let go of Nadine only to wipe
away the tears and quickly replace her hand.

"The baby's fine," She muttered.

I felt horrible. My conscience whispers, *Had
you not been doing something you had no
business... Maybe you could have helped her!*

She tries to talk, but I tell her to save her
strength.

"You just concentrate on getting well. We
have all the time in the world to talk." In agreement
she nods her head; a tear falls from her swollen eye
as she grabs her stomach.

"Do you want me to call the nurse?"

Nadine shakes her head "no".

The silence in the room is deafening. I want
to tell her to leave that sorry punk-ass man. They
have been together since high school. Stewart is
Nadine's first and only love. Devoted to her family,
she would do anything to keep it together, even if it
meant losing her life.

"Boys need their father." This justifies why
she stays with Stewart because they do adore him.
He takes them fishing, taught them both how to ride
their bikes, and takes them to all the sporting events
in town. He does spend a lot of his time with his
boys.

She would never want to take them away
from him but she has to. He's a great father and a

good provider but another baby is just not in his plan. An abortion is definitely not in Nadine's plan, so here we are again.

Miss Kim

Every other Saturday, I help my father at his hardware store. I've been helping him since I was able to talk. I love spending time with him. When we are working together in the store that's "our time." Many of my father's customers are regulars, so they have known me all of my life.

It is a typical day. We are open for the day's business. My dad loves playing the golden oldies on the radio. He tries to sing every now and then. I laugh at him because he doesn't know the words to any of the songs.

I take my post behind the counter. I like being there. Not so much at Mrs. Cheryl's store but here I love it. All while growing up, I sat behind the counter and ran the register. I wouldn't let Stephani run the register. That was always my job. Stephani was in charge of balancing the books and the money. She loved her job too. That's how we learned math, working in the store. I love counting the money when the shop closes. Me and dad bet to see if the cash drawer is short or over. We both lost quite a few bets over the years.

My father schooled us on everything about the business. I know his routine like the back of my hand. I can tell where everything is with my eyes closed. I know how to use most of the appliances and tools. My father told us he wanted us to keep the store running if anything should happen to him. He wanted us prepared.

I'm so proud of him. I admire his ambition to do something that most told him he couldn't do. He takes care of his family, and has been running a successful business for the past 30 years. I want that for myself.

I can set my watch by Mr. Daniels. He

comes in every Saturday at the same time pretending to want something. My father thinks Mr. Daniels really needs these tools. Actually, he has a little crush on me, so I flash him a little cleavage every week.

The store bell rings when Mr. Daniel's leaves the store. It rings again immediately.

I'm trying to see who just walked in. We know most of our customers. It's unlikely someone would come in and not acknowledge us. I only caught a glimpse, but I know I haven't seen him before. I pull my baseball bat closer to me. My father rarely comes to the front when I'm working. He uses his Saturday to work on the inventory. Stephani doesn't work in the store anymore.

The stranger is now in the middle section of the store. I have a clear side view of his towering presence in the distance. He stands tall in his overalls, work boots, with a hardhat under his arm. He is bald, a light carmel-chocolate complexion, and an athletic build. I notice the muscular indentions in his left arm. His chest sticks out as if he's holding his breath. I'm looking at him while he's looking at the shelves. He looks like he works out regularly. His ass is beautifully sculpted. Man can never go wrong with a tight ass, but it is clear my mystery customer doesn't know where to look to find what he wants. I will wait until he comes to me.

Within minutes the stranger is ready to check out. Now, I'm face-to-face with him. My heart starts beating a little faster but I keep my composure.

"Did you find everything ok?"

His skin is smooth and his eyelashes are long, "Yes. The ol' man helped me out."

"That's my daddy. You say you want to mount a medicine cabinet?"

"Yeah."

"Well, the clasp you have will hold, but for a more firm grip you should try the older model we have in aisle two."

"Oh, really?" The stranger spoke with sarcasm. "No, that's okay. I'll just stick with what I have."

I'm offended by his sarcasm. I ring up the purchase without saying a word. Customers always ask my father about everything. Whenever I try to help, the men never take me seriously. They figure since I'm a woman, I don't know what I'm talking about. My father always agrees with me, and the customer leaves with what I suggest anyway. Well, today I decide this fine ass customer is right and ring up his total.

"That will be $20.57," I'm smiling and flirting.

The vision of magnificence standing before me hands me a check, I have to ask for ID. His name is Christian D. Mitchell. His address reveals he didn't live far from the store. Three years older, 6'2, weighs 200 pounds with the longest lashes. The check has a company letterhead that reads Chris D. Mitchell Construction.

Damn! He's fine and has his own company, I'm thinking to myself as I hand the ID back. I finish the transaction and give the gentleman his receipt.

"Remember to keep this; you will need it when you return these clasps."

"Yeah, ok. We'll see," He says and walks toward the door.

"Yeah, we will," I watch him disappear

Miss Kim

from my sight.

It's lunchtime. Sakoya and I are in the Pancake House waiting for a table. She starts in with her conversation.

"Hope we don't have to wait that long, I'm hungry!"

I'm looking around the room trying to find a table.

"Girl, I'm glad you asked me to breakfast. It's been awhile since we've hung out together. You're always working. You should have gotten your promotion by now. What's up with that?" Sakoya's mouth was all twisted.

"This time next year I will get it. I'm just trying to learn all I can so I will be ready for it. Right now, I'm just helping my boss with the extra hours. Nadine is still on sick leave. Mrs. Cheryl let me have today off."

"Whatever happened to that white chick? What is her name? Is she still with her boyfriend?" Sakoya's questions never stop.

"Nadine? Girl, let me tell you. You ain't gon believe it, I feel awful. I talked to her yesterday. Well, I've talked to her everyday since she's been out the hospital. Anyway girl, Nadine said she was preparing a special romantic evening for her and Stewart. It was something she had been planning for a while. Knowing he had to work until six, she called him at the factory asking him to come straight home after work. Her excuse was the sink was stopped up in the kitchen, and she needed him to fix it. The boys helped her with all the dusting, cleaning and mopping. She lit candles and had music playing in the background. The day started off so nice then it just went horribly wrong."

"What happened? What went wrong?"

Sakoya leans in.

Well, after the boys helped her clean, she arranged for them to spend the night with their cousin, Billy. She cooked all Stewart's favorite foods, even got the recipe for pumpkin pie from his mother. (His mother and Nadine do not get along). She put on something sexy, dimmed the lights and waited." I took a breath.

"She probably still looked like a Barbie doll pregnant and all," Sakoya remembers Nadine from Applebee's.

"He didn't come home, so she thought he had to work over. After falling asleep on the couch, she heard a loud crash. She says she was nervous instantly. She looked out the window and saw that Stewart had been drinking again and drove his truck over the mailbox. She told me, he could barely stand when he got out the truck and that he cussed out the mailbox for being in his way. When she heard key in the door, she pretended to sleep on the couch, and hoped he wouldn't bother her. She said he came in cussing out the mailbox. So she jumped up and tried to talk calmly to him asking him, "What's the matter honey?"

Stewart asked her,"What the fuck do you have on?"

She said, before she could finish Stewart slapped her across the face making her fall back on the couch. She said she buried her face in the couch and got into the fetal position to protect her stomach. She said he grabbed a handful of her hair...You seen how long her hair is, right?"

"Yeah girl, I saw it. What else?" Sakoya was into this story.

"He pulled her off the couch into the kitchen by her hair then he saw all the food and candles with the table set for two…" I paused.

"Girl what?"

"He asked her where the guy was. He thought another man was in the house! So girl, he kicked Nadine in her back with his steel toe boots! She said he started yelling at her saying, "You cheatin' on me now. Bitch! I'll show you!"

"She said, he snatched her from the floor and began smashing food in her face. He flipped the dining room table over scattering food all over the place. He pushed her to the floor and asked her again, "Where is he whore! I know he's here!"

"She said, he grabbed more hair, dragging her through the apartment, going from room to room looking for a man in the house. When they got to the boys room and saw they weren't there either, she said that really set him off even more. She said she tried to get away, but he had her hair, yelling, "Where are my boys? Why ain't they here!!!"

"She told me she was scared to say anything because whatever she said it would be the wrong answer. She said he threw her against the wall busting her lip and nose.

"Oh my God!" Sakoya is covering her mouth with her hand in disbelief.

She said he turned his back to look in the closet for the boys and that's when she spotted a baseball bat in the corner behind the door. She grabbed the bat and hit Stewart in his back with all the strength she had. He fell to the ground. She hit him again in the head and again in the balls. That's when he fell unconscious. She said she grabbed an overcoat and ran to the neighbors' house to get help. They let her in, and locked the door. She begged to use the phone. She said she dialed my number then fell to the floor, unconscious." I was glad to be finished with that story.

"Damn, all that happened Saturday night? So is she doing better now? Is Stewart in jail?" Sakoya wanted to know.

"Well, she finally pressed charges against him, has a restraining order, and is now living with her grandmother. She said Stewart is still calling and trying to get back with her. He's been saying he wants to work things out apologizing to her. He said he had stopped drinking. She says she doesn't know what to do because he loves his boys and wants to see them, and she feels bad keeping them apart." I reported.

"How many months is Nadine?" Sakoya asked.

"She's about eight months, and ready to have the baby. She not going to have any contact with Stewart until after the baby gets here. Nadine thinks once he sees his baby girl, he will get his act together." Im just repeating what Nadine told me.

"Maybe he will, that's horrible, but especially since she is pregnant. Is the baby okay? She should wait 'til Stewart drunk like that again, wait for him to pass out and then just beat the shit out of him and leave. Not to sound cruel or insensitive but that means Nadine will be off on maternity leave soon. You'll be makin' all kinds of money girl! Are you treatin' for breakfast?" Sakoya can always find an angle.

"Yeah, but you treatin'next time." I waved my perfectly manicured index finger in her face.

The hostess came to seat us. I spoke to the gentlemen at the next table. The dining area is small. The server greets us and takes our orders. Sakoya rattles off her order immediately, "I would like scrambled eggs, three strips of bacon, and pancakes. Could you bring hot tea also?"

"Sure."

I order an omelet with grits, sausage, and toast. The server grabs the menus and moves one step to the next table.

"What does your boss think about Nadine?" Sakoya is still inquiring.

"She wants her to get back on her feet and leave Stewart for good. That's why she hasn't fired her or replaced her because she knows Nadine is good people and she wants to help her."

"Your boss sounds like a cool woman from everything you've told me about her."

"I know girl. She is so sweet. You should see her house! Her shit is plush! Her driveway heats up so they never have to shovel snow. You know that is pimp shit!" I was joskin' a little bit.

"Ya'll have gotten kinda close, huh?" Sakoya has a twinge of jealousy in her voice.

She had no idea how close we truly were. I would never be able to tell her or anyone about Mrs. Cheryl. How would I explain something like that? I just continue talking like nothing's going on.

"She even took me to her private members only club "Serenity Gardens." I was bragging. Every lady wants to be a member in this prestigious, upscale women's society.

"Girl, shut up'! You got to have paper to be a member of that club!" Sakoya's mouth dropped wide open.

"She took me as a guest, honey. They got everything there. Whatever you want, it is there. I was so amazed, and girl, guess what...no men allowed! I take that back. The only men there are those who work there and security. They wait on you hand and foot. You should see these beautiful older women with their fine diamonds and pearls. All dressed in designer clothes driving the most expensive cars. They got it goin' on. Most of 'em retired. Mrs. Cheryl knows everybody in there. She introduced me to many of her friends. She was telling me a little about each lady there.

The older ladies are members. You have to be at least thirty-five to fill out the application. Their staff is younger women at least twenty-one and drop dead gorgeous, not an ugly bitch in sight, and they had to be referred by an elder member. They have to pass a rigorous training course and sign a contract." I dished everything I saw.

"Damn! What did you do when you were there?" Sakoya hung onto my every word.

My mind flashes back to the tranquil room. Soothing music plays softly. Aromas from the many candles relax and calm my mind while the "supplement" given to me before entering the ultimate massage room relaxes my body. I lay there motionless letting the peacefulness wash over me as two women massage my naked body.

"Mrs. Cheryl is taking tennis lessons, so I watched that for awhile and then just walked around, and talked to a few women. We got full body ultimate massages after her lesson, and we left."

"Ultimate massage? Oooh, I need one of those!" Sakoya closed her eyes as if she could feel the oil running down her back.

However, Sakoya had no idea what a full body ultimate massage meant at Serenity Gardens. Of course she's thinking of a regular body massage like on TV, but that's not what she would get at this place. I couldn't tell her about the massages we received. One woman worked the left side of my body and the other worked the right. They have a closet full of tools or toys they use, feathers, oils, hot rocks and blind folds but mostly they use their hands and fingers rubbing, touching, tickling. What makes it ultimate is the one tool she would not expect, their mouth.

I couldn't tell Sakoya that after my facial treatment the attendant blindfolded me before massaging my neck and shoulders. Starting from my fingertips, two women worked simultaneously back to my shoulders. I was so relaxed and at ease. My thoughts drifted as if at sea. I could feel my body releasing tension as they stroked my neck. They massaged my breasts with warm hands, playful tongues, and sucking lips.

How could I tell her, after my Brazilian bikini wax, the woman gently washed and manipulated my bare baby-like privates with her fingers making it moist and wet then a naked Mrs. Cheryl came in my room to finish the job with her mouth. How could I tell her I enjoyed it all?

"Girl, Mrs. Cheryl says the club is famous for their massages. She says that's the main reason most women become members."

The food has arrived. It smells and looks delicious. We say our prayers with forks already in hand. After taking a few bites of her food, Sakoya asked about Mrs. Cheryl's husband.

"Now, that I don't know much about. I know his name is David. She doesn't talk about him much. I think he is older than she is. She's not happy in her marriage. I do know that."

"Wow, you would think someone with all that she has would be the happiest woman on earth," Sakoya shoves eggs in her mouth.

"You never judge a book by its cover. That's what they tell me."

The server comes over and asks is everything ok. We assure her everything was fine. Sakoya needs more hot water for her tea.

"Here I am running off at the mouth. What's going on with you? I haven't heard any of your new business. Spill it." I was tired of answering all the questions.

Sakoya can't wait to reveal her news, "Well, you remember the guy I told you I met at the club Quentin?"

"Yeah, I remember."

"Well, he was in town last weekend and came over."

"What do you think about him?"

"He's nice enough. We had good conversation over dinner. I know he's a loner because he's a driver. We played miniature golf and girlllllll.... I tried to send him into spasms!" Sakoya cackles loud at her own remark.

We were laughing and the clowns dining close by started laughing too because they were listening in on our conversation.

"That's right. He's a trucker. How long has it been now?" I had forgotten.

"It's been about two months... I know I said I was going to wait until the right man came and we established a stable relationship but he was the man I wanted. Dammit! I couldn't wait any longer! I think I did alright... I went a whole two months."

"No you didn't! You just gave Jason some two weeks ago!" I had to burst her little bubble.

"Oh yeah... I forgot about that. He don't count and Quinn wasn't here. Anyway, I waited two months."

"Quinn? That's what you call him? How was it?"

"The brotha came too fast!!! He couldn't help it though 'cause I was puttin' it down. He in love already, girl. That's why I keep Jason around for dudes who don't quite have the skills just yet!!" Sakoya cackles again.

This time Sakoya heard the guys laughing too.

"They can hear you girl."

"For real?" Sakoya whispers nervously.

I wink at my best friend to let her know I'm 'bout to act up, and she better roll with me. I spoke clearly so the men could hear me.

"Honey, that's a shame! I hate when they cum so fast, did you cum?"

"Girl naw, how could I with *Speed Racer.*"Sakoya follows my lead.

"Next time he comes fast like that don't worry about it. Just go take a long hot shower." I knew this would get the men's attention.

"A shower for what?"

I lean in close as if to whisper to Sakoya while making sure the men at the other table can hear me.

"Honey, I lather my body with my favorite shower gel. I take my time, so I can feel the soapy bubbles tickle my skin."

Sakoya stops eating and the two men are sitting still as if posing for a picture.

I speak slowly, seductively painting a picture of eroticism.

"The bubbles caress my breasts as the water races down the nape of my neck and back."

Both men sit up in their chairs at the same time. Their grins appeared slowly while listening.

They can't believe what they're hearing yet still listening for more. I notice the silent, motionless men at the other table, so I continue.

"Then I take my showerhead and adjust the water pressure to slow and hard. I let the water trickle down the middle of my breast, down my stomach, and between my legs."

Sakoya picks up a piece of bacon and begins chewing it as if she were watching a porno. She listens carefully trying not to miss an iota of information. I have everyone's attention, so I go on with my teasing tale.

"Then I position the warm, spouting water to hit my spot.... Oooh girl!!! It feels so gooood!! It's like thousands of tongues licking' me over and over and over... Girl, I cum so hard I can feel the juices run down my legs! My whole body is paralyzed with pleasure. One time I almost fell and bust my ass in there, lost my balance."

"Oh, my god! I need to get me one of those too! You be having all kinds of fun!" Sakoya whispers excitedly.

Turning towards the two men, I said, "Good morning gentlemen."

Both men responded at the same time, still chuckling over what they overheard. As they were leaving, one of them turns to me whispering, "Girl, you shouldn't talk like that. You could hurt somebody."

I look him down and halfway up and respond, "That somebody must be you from looks of it!!"

He shoves his hand in his pocket and walks out.

Sakoya and I continue catching up on the latest gossip.

"So what's up with you and Freddie?"

"Speaking of cuming too fast!" We bust out in laughter again annoying the patrons sitting on the other side of us.

"Well, I don't get a chance to see him much because he is so busy with school and his ministries. He spends much of his time at Rev. Bookers' house studying. They have become close since Freddie's trial sermon last year."

"Have ya'll been together again since the first time?"

"No, we haven't. He wants to concentrate on his studies. He says I am a distraction, and he must stay focused. He says he has something important he wants to talk to me about tomorrow night."

"What do you think that's all about?"

"I don't know, but I'm excited. Maybe he wants to propose to me!"

"Girl, if he's not tryin' to have sex then you know he's not tryin' to get married. Let's be real."

"You don't know! I'll let you know after we talk."

Sakoya always keeps it real with me. I love that about her, but at the time when she's keeping it real, it pisses me off.

"Check please."

Miss Kim

Normally I would be shooting pool with Stephani but I cancelled the match because of my dinner date with Freddie. I've been on edge since he spoke of his important news.

"What is so important?" Maybe he wants to take our relationship to the next level. I'm not sure what the next level is, but I got my nails done just in case. "Maybe something major happened at school, and he wants to share that with me." If that's the case, he would've told me by now. I have a feeling it is considerable news because he sounded nervous and anxious when we discussed the dinner plans over the phone. He has postponed this dinner three times already, whatever the news, I'm ready.

"Hello."

"Hey, 'Koya girl?"

"Hey what's up? You there yet? You got there quick." Sakoya is rattling off many questions as usual.

"I'm here. I'm sitting in the parking lot of the restaurant."

"What's wrong?"

"Nothing, I'm just sitting and gathering my thoughts." I was a nervous wreck.

"Do you see his car?"

"Yeah he's here…I see my sister's car here too. She and Brandon must be having dinner tonight of all nights. My insides are shaking."

"Just take a deep breath, go to the ladies room, and check yourself out then you should feel a little better. You looked great when you left here, so what are you afraid of? That's great your sister is there to witness the proposal. He probably called her so she could be there." Sakoya was right.

"What if he asks to marry me for real? I

don't know if I'm ready to take that step."

"Dani, stop jumping to conclusions. You don't know what it is. Anyway, I thought that's what you always wanted, to marry *Freddie*. That's all you've talked about since you were ten, marrying *Freddie*. You haven't dated anyone seriously because you said *Freddie* was the only man for you. Girl, get off this phone and go get your ring!"

"Thanks 'Koya. I'll call you later."

"Good luck."

Just before I get out of my car I say a silent prayer, "Jesus, I don't know what this is all about but you do. Whatever it is, please help me. Amen."

Inside the restaurant

Stephani raises her menu high in the air to hide her face when she sees me come in the restaurant. It's obvious she doesn't want to be seen, so I just walk by like I don't see her. I can't believe she's here either and with another man. I definitely will find out what the deal is, as soon as I find out what the deal is with Frederick.

He is sitting in the corner of the restaurant. The ambiance is something out of a magazine. Every table supremely set, with white lace tablecloths, and a small votive candle. From the high ceilings, hang the most exquisite crystal chandeliers. They present just enough light to accompany the candles. The restaurant has beautiful plants and breathtaking floral arrangements precisely placed. The flowers provide a sweet smell that flood through the air. The waiters and hostess' were poignantly dressed with warm smiles to welcome.

Frederick stood to his fee,t when I arrive at

the table, giving me a kiss on the cheek.

While I am taking in all the wonderment of the posh Cabaret, one waiter and one hostess came to our table. They have glass hand bowls filled halfway with soapy water. Each attendant presents the bowl hand level, one to me and one to Frederick. I am stuck because I don't know what to do. I watch Frederick as he dips both hands into the soapy water. There is a clean hand towel draped around the hostess' arm. She then presents the towel for him to dry his hands. I follow his lead and dip my hands into the warm soapy water and smile.

This is high-class shit! I'm thinking to myself as I dry my hands, *Now I will have clean hands when he slides on the ring*. My mind is running rampant with euphoria.

"Dani?"

I slip into a daze as I replay our relationship in my head. Frederick was my first crush, first kiss, and first dry hump. A sly grin came over my face as I reminisce. I remember the two of us trying to "do it." Neither one of us knew what to do, but that made it all the more fun.

The amusement park was our first date. He tried to win the biggest stuffed animal for me. His jump shot only awarded me a midsize koala bear. He didn't want to give me such a small bear, but I gave him the biggest hug and kiss, and he knew it was all good. We were sixteen and in love.

"Dani! What are you going to order?"

"I don't know. What do you suggest?"

"You go ahead and order what you like. I'm not hungry."

"What's up? You ask me to meet you. You haven't said two words to me since we've been here, and now you want me to eat alone!! What's going on? Please tell me. You been acting strange for the last month or so...spill it!"

Forget the small talk; I'm ready for the proposal and can't wait. I want to know, got to know. The mixture of my enthusiasm and his stalling is making me crazy with curiosity. I can tell by his body language he is tense, tense as hell! He is going to pop the question. I'm sure of it.

Oh my God! He is really going to ask me!!! I try to play it cool and calm myself.

"Calm down...Breathe," I'm coaching myself.

But the butterflies, oohh the butterflies!!! I gotta pee. I think my unsettling behavior alerted my date.

"Please calm down," Frederick reaches for my hand.

His touch calms my nerves. I'm able to focus on him and what he's saying, but still, the butterflies multiply, and my bladder is on overload.

"You are making this so hard for me."

"O.k. Baby, let me calm down, please forgive me... Now go ahead and say what you want to say, sweetheart."

Complete silence falls over the table. Frederick slowly pulls his hand away, looks me in my eyes, and began speaking.

"Dani, I've loved you all my life. There has never been any other woman for me. I never wanted any other woman," He is making small gestures with his hands.

I feel goose bumps all over. We are definitely on the same page. I'm shaking my head in agreement, urging him to go on.

"I didn't think anyone could come close to the bond we share. You mean so much to me. After high school, you left and went into the Air Force for four years. I went to college for four years. I have only two classes left in Seminary, and I will have my degree. During that time, I met new people. I know you met new people. I've experienced a lot... We both have... I..." His sentence fell short. He starts again.

"When we started seeing each other again, I thought everything would fall back into place just like in high school, but it didn't for me."

Instantaneously the butterflies stopped dancing. My smile slowly fading.

"Like I said. I never allowed myself to love anyone *but* you, and I've come to realize there may be someone else..."

I no longer have to pee. The silence in the atmosphere is piercing with the echo of "someone else." Frederick's words are confusing. He isn't making sense to me. He remains calm while speaking.

"Someone else. There is someone else?" I can feel a sea of tears rushing my eyes. If I blink, they will surely fall like a thunderous monsoon. I can't believe what I'm hearing.

Frederick handed me his neatly folded napkin waiting patiently for me to regain my composure before he continues.

"I couldn't tell you this over the phone. I wanted to tell you face to face. We have been friends too long for me to do it any other way. Dani, I do love you. It's just we have grown apart, and I feel we need to move on with our lives. I never meant to hurt you... It's hurting me as well. We have been in each other's life almost *all* our lives. Don't you want to experience more?"

"NO," The lump in my throat is blocking

my speech. I feel uneasy, nervous. I try to stop the tears but they keep falling. I feel stupid thinking he was going to propose, "Please excuse me I need to use the ladies room."

I turn and take one last look at him square in his eyes. I love him so much. Instead of going to the bathroom, I head for the coat check, collect my ankle length trench leather coat, and left the restaurant.

Once inside my car, the tears were nonstop. My nose stops up and the lump is still there, stuck. "Someone else" is still ringing loud in my ears. I have to get out of here. The engine revved and the music plays, LTD's, <u>Back in Love</u>. I turn that shit off so fast and peel rubber.

Is he for real? This is not happening; my mind is crazy with emotions. I am not prepared for this. I use the napkin still in my hand to wipe the snot from my nose. I rehearse everything Frederick said to me. The words are still unbelievable.

"How could he do this? I'm the one who loves him."

The replays in my mind were brutal, over and over "someone else" and "move on with our lives" ringing louder and louder. I feel like my head is going to burst like a watermelon smashed by a sledgehammer. I hit the steering wheel hoping to awaken from this terrible dream.

My speed increases on a dimly lit unfamiliar road. I don't know how I got on this street. I'm confused, lost, and don't know where to turn. I smash on my brakes and veer off into a ditch. The car comes to an abrupt stop. My vision is somewhat clear. I still don't know where I am, but I'm okay. "Thank You Jesus!!! Jesus! Jesus! Why is this happening to me!" I reach for my phone.

Miss Kim

"Hello, can you please come and get me?"

Miss Kim

The first Sunday of December and the first snow of the season is falling. The wind is still, the air crisp, and chilling to the bone. Branches are bare of leaves now being outlined with pearly white snow.

Nestled in my warm bed, I don't feel like church today. My head is throbbing, throat sore, eyes puffy; no way am I going. Not to mention, the love of my life dumped me. The memories of the night before were still echoing in my mind. The tears start again, rolling slowly over my nose. I can't stop thinking about it. My phone rings.

"Hello?" I tried to clear my throat, so I wouldn't sound like I felt.

"Hey girl, what happened last night? I tried to call you. You must have had a wonderful time. I'm so excited for you. Tell me everything!!! Was he there waiting for you..."

"'Koya, please shut up for a minute!!!!"

"Damn! Why are you so rude!! I just wanna know girl. I been waiting all-night to hear the great news. How big is the ring? Did he get on..?"

Before my inquisitive friend can finish her sentence, I hang up. The tears were on their way full speed. I know she will call right back, so I turn the volume off on my phone and down on the answering machine. I need a shower.

"Mommy, where you?" Manasha has come into my room.

"Good morning to you Miss 'Nasha."

"See, me pretty," she turns around in a circle, so I can see the dress she has on. It is backwards, zipped half way in front, her shoes are on the wrong feet, and her tights are not pulled up properly. She is a cute little mess.

"Oh yes, mommy's little lady is beautiful. Where are you going today looking so lovely?"

"I going to church. You going too?"

"Yes, I'm going too." Then I remember my car accident and went to use the phone. I have more messages on my recorder. I'm sure most of them are from SaKoya.

"Hey, Sis. I'm glad I caught you. Can you come and pick me and 'Nasha up for church?"

"Yeah, but why aren't you driving your car? Why weren't you driving last night when you came and got Nasha?"

"I'll tell you about it later. How long will you be?"

"Where is my baby? Is she all right? I'll be there in 20 minutes. Tell me what? What's wrong? Are you all right?" Her questions came faster than SaKoya's.

"She's right here. She's fine, but we don't have time for all that. Just come and get us."

We were late for church because Stephani would not leave until I told her everything that happened the previous night. What she really wants to know is if I'd seen her with some man in the restaurant, so I tell her everything. When I finish, we were both crying.

My sister starts handing out her advice. I know she means well, and I know everything she is going to say, but right now at this moment, I really don't want to hear it. Let me wallow in my misery here at church.

"The man will come eventually. You need to prepare for the future of you and 'Nasha. Focus on that and each day will get easier, trust me."

The words sound good coming out but Stephani didn't even believe them. That advice never helps her when she cries for a baby every night, and her husband is off working all the time. She is in that huge house with Constance, the maid. Nevertheless, she has to give her little sister some hope that it will all work out.

"Let's go to church, pray about it, and let the Lord handle the rest."

"He's going to be at church today. I don't think I can stand to look at him. I don't know Stephani when I see him I won't be able to handle it."

"He's not the reason you come to church is he?"

"No."

"Well, you can't let him keep you from receiving your blessings. Look at it like this Frederick came out and told you to your face. He isn't trying to lead you on, and he is being honest. You can't fault a man for being honest."

"Stephani, he made love to me making me feel like we were going to be together. We hung out together, shared secrets, and we made plans."

As I am ranting and raving all while whispering, my memories come flooding back. I recall him saying he loves me, but he never said he was *in* love with me. His plans always included finishing Seminary, but he never spoke of us being together as a couple. He never said he wanted someone else before. Come to think of it, he could have always had someone else. I'm the one who chose to believe my own fantasy which includes me being the first lady of some church here in the community.

"Maybe I'm the one doing all the planning and sharing all the secrets with myself. It's me telling him I love him all the time."

Reality makes me want to turn back and go home, but I know in my spirit, "This too shall pass." With time, I will get over the love of my life, but until then, I have to put on a brave face and walk tall.

Never let 'em see you sweat, I coach myself waiting for the usher to open the door. It's show time. Forgive me Lord. I know he will see me as soon as I walk through these doors. He probably thought I would stay in bed, eating Oreo cookies with the ice cream to match, watching lifetime all day, and letting the devil take my joy; a serpent like Frederick St. James.

With my head held high in my Sunday's best, I stroll with Stephani and Manasha to our pew. He's up there fumbling with his bulletin trying not to stare. He can't keep his eyes off me. I ignored all his calls last night. I left him sitting there waiting on me to return from the ladies room. Dog!

I see the beads of sweat forming across his head. He can't even sit still. Just staring pleading for forgiveness with his eyes. I want to pour acetone in his eyes right now. Pig! *Forgive me Lord.*

All the announcements have been read. The organ hums softly, "No Weapon formed Against Me." This is what I need right now to help lift my spirits. My sister held my hand knowing how I was feeling right now. She has been putting me at ease all my life, like a second mother. Often times, I went to my sister before of our mother.

I can feel the words in my spirit. My sister is right. You can't fault a man for being completely honest. I could tell it wasn't easy for him to tell me something like that, plus it's not like he's the only one I'm seeing, but he is the one I've loved and trusted all my life. I don't know if I will ever love someone completely like I loved Freddie.

"If Frederick broke up with me then there is someone else better than him that God has for me."

I do believe, so I have to have faith, but it still hurts so badly. I'm being tested. I glance his way, and there he is sitting there as if nothing happened last night, reading his bulletin so nonchalant. This is a hard test. My pressure is rising.

"He doesn't care about anyone but himself. Selfish bastard!" I can hear these words in my mind. I stop singing.

He knew he wanted to see "someone else" all along. He wasn't talking about "someone else" when we made love. I can't stop listening to the negative words in my mind.

"Look at him with his legs crossed, singing without a care, not an inkling of remorse. How could he do this? What did I do wrong?"

The questions clutter my mind. The more I analyze it the tighter my grip becomes.
Stephani put her arm around me for comfort. Mrs. Alexander, one of the elders of the church, fans me.

"Go 'head baby. Let it out. It's all right."

The choir took their seats and Reverend Booker rose from his chair.

"Saints, before we leave, I have some wonderful news. I know I shouldn't be doing this, my daughter pleaded with me to keep it a secret. We got a few minutes... We are so excited! I can't hold it Saints...Ya'll know I can't hold water!" He laughs heartedly.

The congregation laughs and seems to agree in unison.

"Frederick, c'mon up here son," The elderly

gentleman motions for Frederick to stand next to him. The room is hushed with all eyes and ears focused on the speaker.

I grab my sister's hand again and sat closer. There *he* stood directly in front of me.

"Saints, Frederick has told me he has accepted Pastoral Leadership at Total Joy Baptist Church in Memphis, Tennessee."

The worshipers stand to their feet and clap for their son in Christ. Frederick smiles nervously.

"Wait a minute! That ain't all." The applause stops. Everyone remains standing.

"He has also asked me for my daughter, Chloe's hand in marriage!!! They will move to Tennessee in two months!!"

For a brief moment, hesitation plagues the congregation. All the church members turn their attention to the only two ladies still sitting in the middle row center aisle. They all await my reaction to the engagement announcement.

Stephani and I sit frozen in our seats for a moment. I can feel heat from all the eyes staring. Someone starts to clap from the rear of the church. It suddenly burst into thunderous applause. The organist plays happy music and everyone rejoices in the good news.

"Ya'll c'mon around and shake their hands before you leave. Wish 'em well on their new journey."

I can't move. I am having an out of body experience. I can see myself shrinking from embarrassment. Stephani gathers her bible, purse, and coat. She whispers my name to break the trance.

"Get your stuff. Let's go."

The lump in my throat is back. My head is

hurting, and all I want is to get out of this church. As we walk by, we can hear the whispers and the hushed tones.

"I always thought Frederick and Dani were going to get married," one lady whispered to another.

"Sure happened quick; I tell ya dat," One member said.

Mrs. B's hand is fastened to her mouth. She knew about Frederick and me. She heard all the stories and even gave advice; "wisdom" she calls it.

Stephani weaved her way quickly through the multitude holding my hand. In the midst of rushing, I let go and followed the line of the well wishers headed straight toward Frederick and his fiancé. Conversing members and unattended children blocked Stephani's path; it was too late.

I feel numb on the inside but a brooding anger blankets my mind and body. I never take my eyes off the young handsome pastor. The closer I get, the angrier I become, teeth clinched, and fists tight. Chloe saw me coming; she slipped her arm around Frederick's to get his attention. Sister Ernestine held Frederick's attention. She wants to give the successful Pastor another kiss for luck. She shakes Chloe's hand and moves on.

Here I am standing before the blushing couple. The room fell silent and all moving stopped.

I couldn't speak because of the lump. Tears are falling, and everyone was watching me.

"Dani," Frederick reached out to me.

In an instant, I aim and hurl a large mucus filled spit wad in Frederick's eye. Frederick covered his face with both hands. I charge him headfirst. We fell over a large planter. The podium fell to the ground. Members rushed the Alter, and the Deacons surround the Reverend to remove him from danger. I bit Frederick on his neck; the on-lookers were shocked and stunned. I am suddenly hoisted away, in midair still kicking, crying and screaming, "I hate you!"

I drove straight to my apartment after church. I don't know what's wrong with me! I can't believe what just happened   I keep flashing back to my father carrying me out of the church like a spoiled brat. It makes me shiver with shame. I never meant for all this to happen. I can't stay home alone tonight, so I pack an overnight bag and drive over to my sister's house.

Brandon and Stephani are upstairs, so I find my way to the kitchen. A gallon of Strawberry Shortcake ice cream is in the freezer. Immediately, I know my sister had gone to store and bought it especially for me. In what they call the "quiet room", I sit by the fireplace to warm my feet. Between heapings, I recount the weekend's events. Beginning with what was supposed to have been my marriage proposal, Saturday night at the restaurant. Ending with a restraining order, a trip to the police station, anger management classes, banned from the church until I apologize to the congregation, and have a counseling session with Reverend Booker, not to mention the embarrassment I caused my parents; immeasurable.

Stephani joined me on the floor with a large blanket and a spoon.

"Why didn't you tell me you and Frederick was having dinner Saturday night?"

"I don't know... I didn't want to jump the gun. I wanted to be sure he was going to ask me. Oh, my God!!! What if everyone thinks *we* were going to get married!?"

"Everyone *did* think you two were getting married. Remember you told them and then told them not to tell anyone. They knew you were seeing each other. He watched you from the Pulpit, you watched him, and everybody watched ya'll." Stephani broke it down.

"Then why did this happen?" I leaned on my sister's shoulder.

"I don't know baby, but everything will reveal itself. Just give it some time. I think as your sister, I should have known all about it. You left me out again. I want to be there for you... when you need me. We are sisters, and we have to have each other's back right?"

I snap out of my self-induced trance and look at Stephani square in her eyes. She could tell something was up.

"Yeah Sis, that's right we are... What's up?" My turn.

"Nothin's up...I'm just sayin'..."

"Sayin' what? Tell me."I like putting Stephani on the spot.

"Tell you what? It's nothin."

"C'mon, I need to hear something else. I know you got something you can tell me," My sister squirms when she lies. She can never lie well.

"No, no, I don't have a thing."

"O.k. Tell me why *you* were at the restaurant Saturday night with that handsome, seasoned gentleman!!!" I point my spoon in her face after I lick it clean. Stephani is standing there with her mouth hanging open.

We laugh out loud uncontrollably until we both held our stomachs. Stephani peeks around the corner to make sure Brandon can't hear her.

"First of all, it's not what you think! You make me sick!! I can never hide anything from you! We were just out having a bite to eat. That's all."

"Well, it didn't look like that after you ran out of there like a whore in church."I laughed.

"I don't know why I reacted like that. I guess because I didn't want you to think... Obviously what you're already thinking! He asked me to dinner. I accepted that's it." Stephani shrugged her shoulders.

"Tell me what led up to him asking you to dinner."

"Okay, okay it was about the sixth session. Brandon attended the first two in August then the sessions were interfering with his work, so I was there alone. That was the deal we made. He would go as long as it didn't interfere. At first, I was going to stop going all together, but I decided against it. I liked talking to him. I figured I needed the therapy more than Brandon anyway. You know why is it so important for me to have a baby? Why I feel like I'm going to die if I don't have one soon.

Well this particular day I was nervous. You know how I get when I get nervous; all sweaty. Well, he asked me if Brandon would be in attendance. Usually, I would make up some kind of excuse because I wanted him to think that Brandon wants to work on our marriage. But we both knew he wasn't going to attend again, so I just told the truth and let it all out, all of it! I figured I would never get to the core of my problems if I wasn't honest with myself and Dr. Scott."

"Okay then what?"

Before she starts again, she peers around the corner to make sure we were alone.

"Before I knew it, I had told the truth for

over my allotted time. His secretary had to knock on the door to remind us of the time. He was standing there with her going over his schedule, and I couldn't keep my eyes off him. I don't know what came over me. You know I don't do stuff like that. I've never looked or lusted after any man since I married Brandon. Dani, for an older gentleman, he is not just fine but refined! He's about twenty years older; you know how I like 'em already gray. He's meticulous and educated. He speaks with such clarity and diction. He handles his elderly secretary with kid gloves, so mannerable. He has a birthmark or something near his left eye. It adds to his mystique.

Girl, it was like I was in there salivating over this man! I wanted to lick that scar on his face like Tisha Campbell licked the part in her boyfriend's greasy hair in School Daze!" We laugh so hard and loud after that statement because we both know Tisha put it on ole dude in that dorm room.

Brandon walks in the quiet room. The laughing stopped. We knew he was trying to listen to our conversation.

"What are ya'll two hens in here cackling about? Surly not the display of affection you showed for your Pastor is it?"

"Shut up Brandon! Don't you have another business trip to go on? See ya nosey!"

"Please stop it you two."

He left. She continues after she walks through the halls to be sure again. She didn't take any chances, so she sits close to me and speaks softly.

"So my time has lapsed, and I have to schedule the next session right? He walks me to the door, shakes my hand then our eyes met and locked for a moment. You know that moment when someone looks at you and lets you know they want you without saying a word? Well he gave me that look, twice!

On the way to my car, I realize Brandon hadn't made me feel like that in I don't know how long. It felt good, for real.

So I'm in my car and my phone rings. It's him, and that's when he asked me to dinner. On the very same night, you are there! I told him when I saw you that it was a sign for me not to be there. I told him how I always had to take you on my dates, so I couldn't have any fun."

"You did have fun! It just costs you. That's all." I shove the last heaping of ice cream in my mouth. I couldn't eat anymore. I thought the story was over when she said, "Guess what?"

"So, after I bolt out of there when I saw you, he starts asking all these questions like, was it him making me nervous or was it the fact of someone seeing us together in public that makes me nervous?"

"What did you say?"

"Well, let's just say dinner will be served at his house on Tuesday after our counseling session. I swear we haven't had any other encounters except the one. We are supposef to have this Tuesday. That's it. The story in a nutshell. *You* told me to get a counselor!"

"Don't put that on me. I ain't told you no sucha thang!" I'm mocking the country dialect of our father.

"I said go get counseling not counseled! I hope you know what you're doing. He is your therapist and seeing him outside the office goes against all the rules. You know that, plus you are married."

"I know... I know...Keep your voice down!!" Stephani peeks around again checking for her husband. She goes on, "He listens to me, he understands me, and helps me to understand myself. He listens to me when I talk about having a baby..."

"That's his job, heffa!!!... I know you want to have a baby. I know more than anybody, but that is something only you and Brandon can work out. Believe me, I will be the first to say kick that brother to the curb! But I know how much you love him, so remember that. What if he found out? What would you do then?"

"He's not going to find out anything because there is nothin' to find out! Dr. Scott is harmless. Brandon is going out of town for a couple of days anyway. He will be back Wednesday. No harm, no foul."

"He's harmless all right. What do you know about him?"

"Well, we don't talk about him much...he is a successful doctor and has many awards on his wall. He's had his own practice for eleven years, his wife died some years ago, and he has two grown girls and a son. He works out regularly and is very meticulous."

"Stephani, just be careful. Are you going to go to dinner at his house?"

"Yes Dani, why?"

"I think that should be your last time seeing this Dr. Scott. You really shouldn't go to dinner. Since you haven't become romantically involved, get out now. Stop this now and then you and Brandon need to sit down and talk to each other."

"You are making more of this than it is.

Brandon doesn't want to talk about babies. He talks about work and that's it. Although he was just telling me upstairs, that things were going to change. He said when he gets back he will be the vice president of FloTu."

"Yeah right. Vice president?" I am being sarcastic.

"Really, he designed a hose clamp that will save the company money and time. When he goes on this trip, he will give his presentation on the economical benefits of this clamp and they will have no other choice but to give him the position. He's really excited about this. You should have seen him upstairs, but I think this promotion will do nothing but take him from home even more."

"Just give it a chance. Maybe it will be the opposite since he will be a big Whig now he can take off anytime he wants. How 'bout that?"

"I doubt it. If he's not talking about having some kids when he gets home..." Stephani starts to tremble. I know she's ready to cry. She stands up quickly and bolts to the kitchen. I follow with the spoons and ice cream.

Brandon breezes through the kitchen to get a beer, and he is gone as fast as he came.

"See, that's why I went out to dinner. He's never here, we don't talk, and we have no excitement..."

"Ya'll are always going to dinner parties and whatnot, right?"

"Yeah, but that's all business. I need someone to listen to me besides you and stuffy old ladies at dinner parties."

"Do you want me to talk to him?"

"No! You've done enough for one day!" Stephani walks through to the game room and over

Miss Kim

to the pool table.
    "Rack'em!!"

Miss Kim

The hustle and bustle of the holiday shoppers kept Reed's Greeting Cards busy. It is just a couple of weeks before Christmas, and it seems everyone is shopping in the store. Mrs. Cheryl is putting the last of the decorations on the Christmas display. Anthony is escorting an elderly woman and her packages to her car. Mrs. B. is running the cash register like always. I'm in the back checking the inventory.

I have no desire to be in the front dealing with the public. It's Monday. I considered taking my Christmas vacation early but at the last minute decide against it. I need the money to move to a better apartment. I like being in the back alone, besides I don't want to see anybody from the church. With their snooty attitudes, looking down on me like I'm the only one in life to bite a sneaky preacher! I know many of the Saints are coming today after what happened yesterday. Every time a member shows up, Mrs. B. runs to the back and reports every word to me. She spares no details. She tells it all.

"Hey Dani girl, hi ya doing back here?"

"Hey Mrs. Cheryl. I'm doing fine. Thanks again for coming to get me Saturday night. I didn't know who else to call. I was in bad shape that night...You said your mechanic will have my car fixed by four today?"

"Yeah girl, he's a friend of my husband's. He is great when it comes to cars. He said he'll have it running and looking brand-new. I'm glad you called. It gave us time to see each other."

I know she wants to say much more, but she is trying to keep it professional. Right now, I'm not in the mood for her lesbionic innuendo.

"I don't know how I'm going to repay you, but I will one day."

"Girl, don't worry about it. I'm glad I could help. Are you sure you are all right? I mean you've gone through a lot these last couple of days."

"I'm all right...it's just I thought...well it doesn't matter now. Did I tell you he's marrying the Pastor's daughter?"

"Well, Mrs. B. kinda filled us all in on what happened yesterday. She felt everyone should know why *you* were doing the inventory instead of me. She's concerned about you and your mental health?" We shared a little chuckle. "Anyway, I came back here to remind you about the small business convention in March if you game, we can go. Everyone including myself was so impressed with you at the Atlanta convention. Many of my colleagues have asked if you were coming to this one also. I thought you might enjoy another little vacation, especially since it's on a Tropical Island!"

"Are you serious?" My mouth is wide open with disbelief.

"This one is four days instead of two with all expenses paid. You don't have to pay for anything. Just make sure you bring your bathing suit and party clothes! This time all of our classes and seminars are in the morning. After the last class, we have the rest of the time to ourselves to do *whatever*. There is a formal ball we have to attend on Saturday night. So, what do you think about that?"

"Oh thank you! Thank you! I need a little "me" time to get my head together. Focus on my goals a little harder."

I'm starting to feel better already. I hug my boss so hard I nearly knocked her glasses off.

"Good, then I'll make all the arrangements and let you know," She turns and walks toward her office. I know I made her day also. She has a little pep in her step now. I wish she wouldn't get so excited because that time will be *my* time not our time.

"Hey. I forgot to tell ya'll Nadine had the baby. She had a girl and named her Gabrielle Nicole," I announced.

"Oh that's wonderful! She better hurry up and get back in here. I need some help around here. I'm the boss. We don't work this hard."

I went to the front of the store to share my forgotten news. Mrs. B. was ringing up her last customer for the moment.

"Dani, would you take over for a spell. I need to go the powder room."

"Sure Mrs. B."

Just as I take my position behind the counter, the store bell rings. It's him, the same delicious guy who was in my father's hardware store. He removes his hat, gloves, and wipes his feet on the greetings mat. He never did come back to tell me I was right about the clamp I suggested. His attention is directed toward the get well cards.

I know the store inside and out just like my father taught me. He said, "Know your surroundings and familiarize yourself with detail. You never know when your sight may fail you."

Mrs. Cheryl emerges from the back and immediately notices a flaw in the display. She wastes no time repairing the red nosed reindeer. The store bell rings twice.

A man in a black overcoat, suit and tie comes straight to the counter.

"Excuse me Miss. Is there a Nadine Hughes

working here? It's urgent I speak with her."

After repairing the display, Mrs. Cheryl comes over to the counter to greet the gentleman.

"Good morning. May I help you sir?" Mrs. Cheryl extends her right hand.

"I'm looking for Miss Nadine Hughes. We have your address as the last place she worked. Is she here now?" The man searched the store.

"No, I'm afraid she isn't here today. She's on vacation. May I tell her who's inquiring should she happen to call?"

"No. Thank you for your time," The gentleman left the store.

Mrs. Cheryl, Mrs. B., and I stand wondering what he wants with Nadine. It lasts very briefly. "Well, let's get back to work."

Curiosity makes me wonder about Mr. Delicious. I hesitate before going back to inventory. I watch him secretly. I can tell by his expression. He didn't like the selection of cards.

"May I help you find something?" I ask in my most professional voice.

"Yeah, I'm looking for a card for my mother. I can't find one that says what I want to say."

"Oh, well have you tried these here? I have read a few and the author captures the moment," I show my customer a different section of cards.

"Thanks."

"If there isn't anything here you like, just let me know and I will create one for you."

"Oh really? You can do that?"

"Yeah, sure that's what I do. Take your time."

I went back to my inventory. I don't want to appear pushy or desperate. Anthony is coming out of the men's room when he almost ran me over.

"Aye girl, I heard you going 'round biting preachers, destroying churches, and shit. What's up?"Anthony and his juvenile sarcasm gets on my nerves.

"Shut up! Punk! You don't know shit and stay out my face!"

"Ooooh I'm sooo scared. Girl, you betta back up, before I drop kick you."

He's teasing me trying to make me smile. It's not working today.

"Get away from me!"

"All right, that's enough out of both of you. Get back to work!" Mrs. Cheryl is standing in her doorway.

Anthony was on his way to the front of the store, when he stops then turns back to me.

"Aye, for real… When you gonna let me take you out?"

Before I could really give Anthony a piece of my mind, my phone rings.

"Hello?"

"Dani, he's ready to have a baby!!" Stephani is shouting on the phone.

"He told you that?"

"Nooo, but he keeps saying it's going to be different when he gets back. He knows all I want is a baby, so that's what he means, right?"

"Right, honey oohh I'm so happy for you," I agree with her because I want her to be happy; she deserves it, "See, I told you. You just needed to be patient, even though what's-his-face could have been a little more sympathetic, but you almost ruined everything with the little doctor stunt. Please tell me you are not seeing him anymore?"

"I told him I would meet him tomorrow.

Miss Kim

That's when I'll tell him we no longer need to continue with our sessions. He's such a kind man. I don't want to cancel at the last minute. Dani, I promise I won't stay long. Besides, my husband is coming back to make passionate love to me Wednesday night. I can't wait!!"

"Well, let me stop you there. I'm not trying to hear all that right now. I gotta go back to work. Where is *my* baby?"

"She's with Constance. We left them having lunch in the pool house."

"See ya after work."

It's finally time to call it a day when I get another phone call. It's Nadine. She sounds a little on edge.

"What's going on mommy?"

"Did some man come to the store looking for me?"Nadine starts to cry.

"Yeah earlier. What did he want?"

"Girl, he came over here to serve me papers. Stewart is taking me to court for sole custody of the boys. He feels the boys will have a better life with him and his new wife Rebecca. They have a home in Cincinnati, and they want the boys to move there with them."

"Oh baby I'm so sorry. Please don't cry. Everything will work itself out. What do you think about that?"

"My boys ain't going nowhere! We will be going to court because there is no way I'm going to give him sole custody, Dani!"

"Okay at least we have a starting point. You know what you are not going to do so go from there. What does your grandmother think about it?"

"My grand mother? Why you ask about her?"

"Did you tell her?"

"Yeah, she was here talking to the man that served the papers. She said she knows I love the boys, but sometimes we all need help and maybe it isn't such a bad idea for him to take them until I get back on my feet. She said to try and talk to Stewart and come up with some kind of temporary agreement. She asked me was I going to keep the boys from him."

"Are you?"

"No, you know that's the last thing I want, but I wasn't the one beating on him, coming in drunk at all times of the night, and raising hell because I couldn't cope. Now he got a wife, so I'm the unfit parent? Ain't that a bitch!"

"Nadine, I'm on my way over."

I know she needs me now. That's a low blow what Stewart did. He could have called her first to talk about sharing custody of the boys. He went straight to court. I'm upset myself the more I think about it on the way over.

Her grandmother greets me with a big hug. We can't hug tight because of her Nikon digital camera is in the way. She fancies herself a photographer never taking it from her neck.

She wants me to talk some sense into her granddaughter. She tells me, "Dani, I'm old. I won't be here long, and she has to stand up for herself and her kids. I want the best for all of them, even Stewart. Sometimes we have to sacrifice all we know in order to get what we want and need out of life. That's all I'm trying to get her to see. Do you understand what I'm sayin'? She's in the den."

"Yes I do…Okay grandma."

When I walk into the den, the walls are covered with a plethora of framed pictures. Family portraits placed just right. It's as if their family history is right here displayed on the walls, in curio cabinets, on end tables; everywhere. Some of the pictures were so old and fragile, but Grandma has preserved and kept them like ancient artifacts.

"Hi sweetie, thanks for coming over you really didn't have to."

"You sound like you need someone to talk to about all this, so of course I'm coming over to help. You my girl! Plus I want to see Gabrielle."

"Thank you so much, but can you believe Stewart? Look at these papers. Why is he doing this? She's sleeping in her bassinet. We call her Gabby."

Nadine's beautiful blue eyes fill with tears. She's trying to be brave but Gabby's sudden cry unleashes a flow of teary, snotty emotions. She scoops up her precious baby girl. Instantly, they both stop crying. She walks around the den gently bouncing Gabby over her shoulder.

"Look at this Dani…This was taken when I was pregnant with Nathan. We were so happy. I remember the day I told Stewart I was pregnant with Nathan. He jumped around, picked me up then set me down lightly because he didn't want to upset the baby. I was all of two months," She smiles as she remembers the good times.

"I told you how he reacted when I told him about this last pregnancy. He was livid, 'two is enough' he said. I thought it would all pass but it didn't. It really made everything worse. I never thought we would break up.

I just can't do it Dani. I couldn't get an abortion. It goes against everything I believe in. We were stuck. He didn't want another baby, and I couldn't get rid of one. One time he said we could have another baby later. Later?! Sweetie, I'm pregnant now! That's when the argument started." She put Gabby back in the bassinet but continues to pace the floor.

"He tried to say he didn't know what he wanted to do with his life. Saying he didn't want to stay at the old paper mill. He wanted to do something else, so I asked him, 'What are your skills Stewart? Do you have any talent Stewart?' He never said a word, so I kept on drilling him. You want me to condemn my soul to hell, so you can follow a dream you know nothing about or have skills for? He had a look I'd never seen before and then he hit me in the face."

I can see her body shaking as she relives the painful memory. I don't know what to say or do. All I can do is listen. Nadine is overwrought with emotion switching from tears to anger.

"Of course, since the truth cut him to the core, he retaliated by calling me the town whore, saying I never cared about my soul when I was club hoping every night. He said Gabby probably wasn't his anyway," She curls up on the couch next to me and cries on my shoulder.

"Oh baby, it's okay. He was angry. He didn't mean it. He knows Gabby is his. He just wasn't ready. We all say things we don't mean when we feel defenseless. Stewart had no right to put his hands on you. You did the right thing by having Gabby and leaving him. I'm so proud of you so is your grandmother. She doesn't want you to make any rash decisions. Think about all the stuff you just told me and make a rational decision. It seems awful now, but you can handle this. It took courage for you to leave your high school sweetheart. You stood by your values and put your baby before yourself. The fight is in you. You are not a victim."

It's time for me to get back to my sisters house. Taking one last look at the baby I take a picture with my camera phone to show the gang at work.

"First thing tomorrow I'm calling the child support bureau for all *my* kids. I ain't taking his bullshit no more sweetie! If it's a fight he wants, it's a fight he will get! Shiiiittt, fuck Stewart!"

"Damn girl! You soundin' more like a black girl everyday!"

Because of the fiasco with Frederick and the church, my life has been all work and no play. I have buried myself in work, anger management, and self pity. I barely notice the holidays. I didn't get any real Christmas presents. The only new resolution I have is to get it together. My life is in a rut right now.

I'm not dating anyone, no new flings on the side, well maybe a tune up every now and then, but nothing to write home about. I am staying focused on my dreams of owning my shop.

Three months have passed and it has finally come, the small business convention on Taveuni Island. You can imagine my excitement level when I finally get to the airport ready to board a plane taking me to the third largest Island in Fiji. This may be job related, but I will definitely have some fun before I leave. I may never come this way again.

I check my bags in and wait for Mrs. Cheryl to arrive. I already called her twice, no answer.

"Danielle Thompson...Danielle Thompson please report to Gate twelve."

"It figures. She's here already," I make my way to the gate.

"Hi, Cheryl. I'm standing down in the lobby waiting on you. How long you been here?"

"I like to get here early, so I can read the paper and have a drink before I get on the plane."

Mrs. Cheryl's intentions are always good but she tends to over do it sometimes. I'm ready to fly in my jeans and nice blouse while she has overdressed in her Prada pantsuit with matching stilettos and clutch. She never goes anywhere without her black cat glasses. She didn't even have a paper.

"Are you afraid to fly?" I quizzed my boss.

"No. Not afraid, but I need a little something for my nerves, and my ears, and my stomach."

The flight has been delayed an hour, so we have plenty time to catch up on all the news. We take our bags to the restaurant in the airport. We sit facing our gate. Mrs. Cheryl starts the questioning.

"What do you plan to do with all the information you will learn at this convention? I mean everybody just kept asking me about you after that first one girl. You really make an impression the way you handle yourself. For real girl... I can see it. Everybody sees it, so work it girl!"

In my most proper English I spoke, "I intend to do just that... Work the shit out of it! They shant know what hit them once I get through. By the time the convention is over, I will know everyone who is anyone, and if I don't know them, I'll know their assistant or at least have their card. They don't know it yet but they will help me get started. Don't let there be some little ol' man in charge. He's first on my hit list!"

"Girl, you are too much."

The boss needs another drink. She almost chokes from laughing. Mrs. Cheryl checks on our flight. There's a gas leak. so we have to board a different plane, which means the flight has been delayed even longer it will be after midnight before we board.

"You wanna drink?"

"Hell yeah. A double! May as well start now before the classes begin because after each class, it's on! Oooh girl, I'm hot just thinking about it, but we may not even make it to the first class because of the flight."

"Well, you better drink up then. I see you have forgotten about you-know-who?" Mrs. Cheryl is trying to pick my brain see if my head is spinning.

"Who Frederick? He's a jerk, and I'm better off without him."

When I talk or think about that awful time, I start getting upset. I didn't come down here to be mad. I will let go of all the bad karma. The fact that it's been three months since I've been to church, and I haven't apologized to the pastor nor ask for forgiveness from the church. I did however graduate top of my anger management class. I've learned to take what happened to me and turn it into something positive. I'm just scared to face the church so I've been putting it off.

All baggage has been loaded onto a fully fueled jet liner. We immediately grab our things. It's hard for Cheryl because she isn't finished with her drink and she wants to carry it on the plane. Mrs. Cheryl politely set her drink down once they told her she would be jailed if she didn't comply with the rules.

I'm both exhausted and excited at the same time. I love flying at night, watching the stars, lights, and seeing the streets at peace. The runway and overhead lights were on in the plane. People were scrambling to get comfortable hopeful to catch a nap before landing.

We follow the flight attendant to our first-class seats. Mrs. Cheryl makes a point of sitting all the way in the back. She says it's more room back there. I sit next to the window. She's up to something. Since there are three seats, I thought she would leave the middle seat empty, so we could put our feet up or our little knick knacks for the ride. No she sat right next to me. I can see it coming now...Drama! She orders another round of drinks promptly.

"Mrs. Cheryl you better slow down 'cause I can't carry you!"

"Worry 'bout your damn self! Who gon carry your fine ass? I'm straight. Don't worry about me. It's Cheryl you know that. So what's this about a new guy in Nadine's life? I don't know all the details. I just overheard ya'll talking in the break room."

I think Cheryl was a spy in her past life because she's always overhearing something. She's feeling real frisky now, starting to talk strange, and is extra nice to me.

"Well, that's all because of me. His name is Calvin Baxter. He was my counselor in anger management classes. I thought him and Nadine would hit it off."

"Did *he* have an anger problem? 'Cause if he did Nadine defini...defin.. Sure don't need *him*. She has a tendency to piss men off."

Her words were starting to run together. Sometimes she's fun when she's loaded.

"No, I already checked. He's a licensed Psychologist. He has his own home, twenty-seven years old, and divorced. He is fine. He has a daughter.

Nadine talks about him all the time. The kids have taken to him. They haven't gotten serious yet, but they spend a lot of time together, horseback riding, bowling, and the whole family goes to the movies every Sunday. I babysat Gabbs while they were gone. She is adorable. Anyway, I was trying to help Nadine. She was so depressed when she received that letter from court."

"What is that all about?" She let out a hideous burp, "'Scuse me."

"Stewart filed for sole custody of the boys stating that Nadine had too much responsibility now that Gabrielle is here. Nadine wasn't having that, so she filed for child support for all the children. When her support was settled, the courts reviewed her case. She proved she was able to take care of her kids, especially since she lives with her grandmother and has a part-time job."

"Where else does she work?"

"The last time she was in the hospital someone gave her pamphlet for battered women. Well, she finally went to get help, and liked it so much she volunteers and answers the phones. I guess the women love talking to her. She spends hours on the phone with all kinds of battered women, counseling or just listening to the horrible stories. They request to speak to her personally...Oh damn! I forgot to tell my sister 'Nasha's shoes are under my bed."

"Your sister always has your baby. I know you're going to hate it when she has her own buddle of joy. No more baby-sitter for you. When is she due?"

"No, I'm not. I'm so happy for her. She's due sometime in September. When she told me, I just started jumping around and clapping my hands. Stephani has wanted this for such a long time."

"What about her husband? How is he taking everything? He didn't want any kids, did he? Stop that girl the next time she walks by."

"You know it's strange. He seems happier than Stephani. It's like the tables have turned. This baby is all *he* talks about. He's already thinking of names. He's ready for their Lamaze classes! I know that Stephani is ecstatic, but there is something wrong...I don't know. Maybe it's just me."

"You know pregnant women get moody, depressed, and happy all in twenty minutes so you know," She reclines her seat and throws her blanket over her.

"I guess. I told her to fix herself up. You know get a facial, manicure, and pedicure whatever. She's just been lying around the house. She doesn't call me as much. The last time she was happy about anything was when Brandon was coming in from an important business trip."

My mind flashed back to her phone call. Stephani had been on that date with the doctor. I distinctly remember her telling me she had an uneasy feeling about the whole thing. She said once she got there she realized she made the wrong decision.

He had the table set with candles lit. She walked in saw the candles and turned to walk out. He blocked her way asking her repeatedly to stay. She made it home, called me, and said that was the last time she would see him again. We hung up.

"Well, that Tuesday she was anxious for Brandon to come home because he was going to be named Vice President of FloTu. He told her he was ready to start a family, and he has held true to his promise. So why is she so unhappy about this pregnancy?" Get me another drink when the waitress comes by."

"She's pregnant so expect that. When you going to fix yourself up? Miss Cupid, Miss Makeover unlimited," My boss jammed her index finger in her ear shaking it up and down. Opening and closing her mouth trying to make her ears pop.

"Fix myself up? Honey, I don't need any fixin'," Checking my compact mirror, the waitress bought my tall Gin and Juice and two Jack and Cokes for Cheryl.

"Where yo man at?"

"Shiiit where your man at! He's certainly not here with you, I am. Besides a man is the furthest thing from my mind. I'm just trying to have some fun. Besides I have some goals I'm trying to achieve, so a relationship will have to wait. Mr. Frederick St. James has taught me well. A man will never have that much control over my life again. It's all about me now. Right now, I'm just kickin' ass and takin' names later!" I mean that shit.

"What about the bald guy that keeps coming to the store? You know the tall, bald guy. He buys the get-well cards all the time. Didn't you say he's been in your father's hardware store too? What about him?"

"Yeah, so what? What about him? He comes to get cards for his mother. She has Cancer."

"You don't think he's coming in to see you?" Mrs. Cheryl continues her investigation. "Didn't you say he asked you out a couple of weeks ago?"

"So, I declined. As fine as he is, I'm sure he has plenty of women to go out with. Look, even if I want to go out with him, now is not a good time. I want to start my line of greeting cards and have my own store by thirty-five. I got shit to do."

"When you complete all this shit, who are you going to share all that happiness with?"

"What you want me to say… You? I know you just trying to get me down here alone with you, away from your husband. I bet you jumped for joy when they told you the conference would be here because you know I couldn't turn something like this down."

"Just bring us two more. No four more of those little bottles and we straight. If you get more, there will be a little something in for you when you get back," My boss was bribing the young flight attendant. She went along with it. Cheryl turned to me and continued, "Well, for real we never get to see each other. I know you have been through a lot these past couple of months. I have kept my distance and given you time to heal from that douche bag you called your man."

"Whatever hater! I truly loved him and you know that. You just wish it were you I'm in love with," I'm straightening my cover so my legs are fully covered.

"You may not be in love with me but you love what I do to you. Do you really think you were going to stop wanting…" She put her hand on my thigh.

"Here you are Mrs. Reed. Can I get you anything else? You have to order now because we are about to change shifts and shut everything down," Her apron is filled with little tiny liquor bottles. She dumps them in the empty first seat and waits for her something extra. Cheryl gives her a hundred dollar bill.

"No, thank you. Could you tell me when will we be landing?" Mrs. Cheryl inquires.

"We should be landing in about an hour and thirty minutes," The attendant leaves.

"Before you go, can you make sure we are not bothered back here. We want to get some sleep before our presentation tomorrow. Make sure all the lights are out, thank you so much," She slips the attendant another bill as she walks off.

Miss Kim

The lights went out throughout the cabin and along the runway. There were a few personal above lights on toward the front of the plane. I can see the attendant asking those persons to please turn their lights out. It's suddenly totally dark in the plane, pitch black in our corner.

Mrs. Cheryl is under the covers, under my skirt, between my legs, licking the lace on Jezebel boy shorts. I tell her to stop but she doesn't. I really don't want her to stop. No one can see her pawing at my panties pulling them to the side. Licking me quietly, like a cat taking a morning bath, each stroke more sensual than the last. I hate that I like it so much. How does she do it so well? My hips move in unison with her exploring, hot caressing tongue. She takes me there; gets me there fast and hard. It's explosive. My body stiffens with waves of pleasure pulsating through my core. I'm addicted to it.

I turn to my boss when I straighten both my panties and skirt. She is finely sitting upright in her seat with her blanket wrapped around her, "Let the games begin!!!"

Our arrangement is adjoining rooms. A single bathroom connects the two roomy bungalows. They are fittingly decorated with fresh flowers, and light pastel colors, the drapes and bed comforter match, complete with a stocked bar, cable TV and DVD player. A veranda with lawn tables and chairs overlooking the water with jaw dropping views of the sunset stretch along both cabins. A hot tub sits in the middle of the veranda to accommodate both rooms. It's down for repairs.

We decide to take a nap, so we can go refreshed for the informal meet and greet. But my curiosity can't resist a quick peek around resort.

The technicians working on the hot tub said it wouldn't be long before they were done. Once they finished, they would fill the tub with water as a courtesy for the inconvenience. That gives me time to look around. I knock on the bathroom door to see if Mrs. Cheryl wants to join me. She is passed out on her bed.

I check all the festivities the resort has to offer. There's boating, scuba diving, snorkeling, none of which I like. I'm afraid of drowning. Line dancing, bingo, bowling, tennis, and karaoke was also available. Everywhere I went there were beautiful chocolate, caramel, and butterscotch men. Even the white men look like they just stepped out of a magazine. Tall, short, slender, and thick I love them all although I do have a small problem with short men.

I smile at all who smile at me as I make my way in and out of the stores and shops. Everyone is so polite and courteous. The natives and all the staff really make you feel like royalty here.

Conversing with the bartender about the resort, he's able to tell me about the activities not listed on the itinerary. He is very complimentary. He asks me would I like to go out after my seminars. He's a decent looking man, but I didn't want to commit to something so soon. I don't know what or who else would come up. I explain to him that I'm here with my boss and want to wait until I confer with her to make sure she has no prior engagements. He understood and told me he would be off his shift at eleven. I return to my room. I only have an hour and a half to nap.

The meet and greet is nothing more than that. The conference room, lined with tables of all you can eat meat, cheese and fruit. There were only a few tables. The intent is to keep moving and interact with everyone. Men and women from all over have come to this small business convention.

Cheryl and I split up once we arrive at the meet and greet. I want to go a little late, so I can make an entrance. Mrs. Cheryl immediately makes her way to the bar and remains there most of the night.

I met and greeted everyone in my sights, gave, and received business cards. There were many faces I remembered from the last convention and they all remembered me. I'm almost sure it was the mauve suit with pearl white lapel that stood out in their minds. I am also amazed at how many remembered my name. It's one thing not to forget a face but almost no one remembers a name. I didn't wear my nametag on purpose. I figure, if they want to know me, they would strike up a conversation and ask.

The conference room is a little crowded. The air-conditioner had gone out again. I'm outside listening to the wind and feeling the breeze from the water crashing against the sand. I check for my boss before I leave. She's in good hands with another conference goer. She looks like she was having a great time.

I spot the bartender from earlier. He's still working, and it is after eleven o'clock.

"Hey, you still here?"

"I'm waiting to see if you're going to stop by," Wiping the counter, the bartender gives me smile.

"Oh, is that right? Well..umm..please forgive me. What did you say your name is?"

"Freddy."

Miss Kim

I walk away as fast as I can. "Lord Jesus!" I was not expecting that answer and it caught me off guard. I'm sure he's nothing like the asshole I left behind, but I'm not sticking around to find out. I go directly to the wet bar next to Mrs. Cheryl. She looks as if she has taken up residency there on that same bar stool.

"I need a double Vodka on the rocks with a splash of lemon, please."

"What's wrong with you? You look like you just seen a ghost," Mrs. Cheryl sips her drink.

"Are you just going to sit at the bar all-night? Have you met anybody?"

"I know most of 'em. I brought you here, so *you* could connect with others in the industry. So you know how to handle your biz..iness. I want you to be suc...cess..ful. I know you think all I want is your body...I do but I really, really, really reeaallly want you to be suc...cesss..ful," Mrs. Cheryl raises her glass to make a toast, "To my successor, I know you will become a great business owner one day soon, cheers."

We touch glasses. I close my eyes and swallow all the clear liquid in the glass.

"Give me another one, just like the other one!" We sing in unison.

I look over to my left and see two fine men looking in our direction. They are from the convention because I see their nametags. They look to be in their late twenties, early thirties, just the way I liked them. I try to be subtle and tell my boss we are being watched.

Mrs. Cheryl dramatically looks around me and wave the men over.

"Hi, How are you? I'm Cheryl Reed of Reeds Greeting Cards. This is Danielle

Thompson."

"Hello, please to meet you. I'm Brock Davidson of Gallant Computers, and this is..."

"William Griffin," The gentleman spoke for himself.

After the introductions, the two men ask us to join them out on the terrace where we all could talk and get to know one another. I explain how I am here trying to learn more about small business and how to start my own the proper way.

Brock tells us of his business, computers. He has had his company for four years. The five foot eleven, dread wearing, slender golfer is single, has one child, and loves to cook. He collects art and volunteers at the boys club in his hometown of Chicago. He's looking for someone to share the rest of his life with. Right now he has "friends with benefits."

He's gentle and thoughtful, the kind of man that listens to you and will take his woman out on a date every week. He's the kind that will go to the grocery store and get you tampons if you run out. He's full of pride and respect and would never let anyone disrespect his woman or family.

His partner William Griffin owns a software store. All the new up and coming software programs coming out "Billy" knows about it. The closely shaven William has a body women salivate over and lips that women watch when he talks. His walk, no other could possibly imitate. He's rough and rugged. I can tell he works out. He's the rebel type, cocky and full of confidence. I'm positive his lovemaking makes women swoon in ecstasy. They would always let him hit it one more time. Dreaming of him will have you touching yourself in your sleep.

Miss Kim

Although he is spoken for, he and his girlfriend have been together for seven years. He would never leave this woman. He admits he "occasionally cheats." Meaning he doesn't cheat with just anybody, she has to be special, equal or better than his girl. She had to be worthy of his indiscretions.

They met through a mutual friend five years ago. The two became close friends, joined forces, and combined companies as equal partners, transforming their "small business" into something more profitable. They had it all work out to the last detail.

William and Brock were good-looking, charming and polite. It turns me on listening to them pitching their ideas and asking our opinions. I feel a vibe from Brock listening to his business deal. We walk to the terrace with the live band playing, everything from New Edition's <u>Mr. Telephone man</u> to <u>La Bamba</u>.

Brock kisses both my hands as he helps me to my seat then Cheryl. He didn't kiss her hands. Before you know it, we're laughing all night long. He told us stories of how he taught his little brother a lesson about stealing his change. By heating the coins with the iron, leave the room knowing his kleptomaniac of a brother would try to take them. Mocking his brothers' reaction to the hot change is priceless. We laugh for a good minute.

Then there is William, a man of few words. He did most of his talking with his eyes. Sexy as hell, wearing a hoop earring, and a diamond stud watch, everything about him arouses the senses. He sits at the table drinking his Cognac smoking a Newport. It's moist between my thighs just watching. He is smooth, but he can't help laughing at his partner. They had a great friendship which made for a better partnership.

Toasting to lasting relationships, we also formed a new partnership which we deemed "The WDBC". It is our first initial from our first names. Right there at the table we exchange full names, phone numbers, and addresses. From this day, whenever one in this group is in need, be it financial, personal, whatever, the remaining three vows to be there for that one, no matter what. That's the pact between us four.

To seal the deal, we lift our glasses shouting, "Hear! Hear!"

I shout, "Hear Yee! Hear Yee!"

Music starts to play softly. The men ask us to dance and we oblige. Not only are they great businessmen but are equally great dancers. Brock can salsa his ass off. William looks sexy doing anything.

Cheryl leaves the dance floor to freshen up her drink so I dance with both men. I have no problem with that. Cheryl is gone a second before she makes her way back to the dance floor. We dance until we can't move a muscle.

"It's getting late. We have classes in the morning."

The men walk us to our rooms as we recap the funniest events of the meet and greet on the way. Cheryl retires for the evening in her room while me, Brock and William decide we aren't sleepy yet. I found a horror movie. Everybody is up for watching it.

William really wants to party more, but we would have to leave the resort. No one knows the way around the island or has transportation. I order popcorn from room service because it looks like we're in for the night.

I turn out all the lights and pull the shades to create the illusion of a movie theater. We were comfortable on the couch waiting for the flick to begin. Thirty minutes into the movie my thrill seekers are asleep. I lay my head in Brock's lap.

"Knock... Knock," I jump up quickly to open the door. No one is there.

"Hey, in there?" More tapping, it's coming from the bathroom door.

My guests hear the tapping, spring up, shuffle for their shoes and out they went. I open the bathroom door.

"Ya'll better get a move on. Classes start in forty five minutes," Already dressed, Cheryl has eaten her complimentary breakfast ready for her second cup of coffee. Miss Perky.

"Oh, I see you had a good time last night. Tell me about it later. Get dressed quickly."

My boss makes sure I'm on time to all my classes. She was the same way at the first convention. This is her passion, and she's excited for me. Wanting me to prosper and carry on the secrets of great businesswomen across the world. Education was first on her list, "knowledge is power" she stresses. Networking and meeting new people is very important. "You'll never know when you'll need them."

My two new friends met me at our introductory class. We check the itineraries to make sure we can meet for lunch.

I have my little tape recorder, so my first-class is a breeze. I'm not sleepy at all. It's after lunch when I feel like someone is standing on my eyelids. I stood in the back of class to stay awake.

My drill sergeant in basic training made me stand in back of the class when I would fall asleep but nothing worked the sleep monster had his way. Class ended and everybody that walked right passed me posted up against the wall, asleep.

I decide to skip the last class of the day and rest up for the tour tonight. I made plans to go with Brock and William on a tour of the Island. There is a tour in the morning also but we will be in class. The brochure describes the night Safari as spectacular because of the lights, moon, and stars. The picture of the night sky was so vivid like something from a movie. Living in the city, I never get a chance to see true nature at its finest.

Mrs. Cheryl attends the last class. She makes me give her the tape recorder so I can at least have the information. She can't believe I skipped the class and now sleeping for a night on the island.

"Did you come here to just party with *two* men or learn something?"

"It was innocent. They were respectful gentlemen. We had a wonderful time although I wouldn't have minded some pole action... Ya know!! I really don't know which one I want. They both look good and have great personalities. I'm trying to figure out which one can really put it down on a sistah!

You should have kicked it with us. I thought you were coming to have some fun too. You just all about the meetings, huh?"

She stands in the bathroom doorway looking at me like I said something foreign, "I thought we were going to hang out and have some fun too." My boss sounds like a wounded puppy wanting someone to pick it up and cuddle it.

"Are you serious? You cannot be serious.

Cheryl we have our fun. That's it. That's all. We agreed that our fun would never mess up our friendship, right? So you saying you can't have fun unless it's with me? Well, that is completely crazy!"

She didn't say another word. Still standing there holding her Pina Colada. I can tell I hurt her feelings, but at this point, I really don't care because she is not keeping her end of the deal.

"That's why you came in here waking me up because you're jealous that I was with Brock and William last night and going out with them again tonight? I thought you had fun last night too, didn't you?"

"Yeah, I had fun last night but…"

"No buts Cheryl. Just concentrate on having a great time. We don't have a lot of time left so let's make the best of it, okay? Do you want to come with us tonight?"

"No."

"Don't hate on me because you trippin'!! When we get back, don't have your lips poked out talking 'bout you didn't have any fun. It's your own fault."

Mrs. Cheryl sips on her giant pina colada, rolls her eyes, and left my room.

Since I'm awake, I call Stephani to check on Manasha. She has dumped all of Stephani's White Shoulders powder on the floor and rubbed it all over her body. I can hear her running through the house.

"Dani, let me call you right back after I catch *your* daughter."

"Okay, but be careful. You shouldn't be chasing her. Get Constance to get her."

Half hour later my phone rings, "Hello?"

"Girl I finally got her! I gave her a bath and

put her in bed. Of course, she is not asleep but she's in bed. I swear she prays for everyone she knows just so she can stay up longer."

"Well, she is a con artist."

"She gets it honestly. Well, lil sis have fun. I'm tired. I'm just going to lay here until Brandon gets back with my macaroni salad, so I'll talk to you later."

"Okay Steph. Take it easy. I love you."

Now that I have talked to my sister, I'm feeling a little better. I have to take a nap so I can be fresh for tonight. Just as I wrestle the crisp, white, clean Royal Heritage sheets over my shoulders, my phone rings again, it's Brandon.

"Hey how you doing? You learning anything on that island?"

"You sound like Cheryl."

"Cheryl?" He didn't know who I was talking about because I never call her by her first name around anyone.

"My boss, Mrs. Cheryl."

"Well anyway Dani, I called because I'm worried about your sister. She just isn't the same. Something is wrong, and she won't tell me what it is. I thought maybe you know something. Has she talked to you at all?"

"I thought I was the only one who noticed it, but no, she hasn't."

"Since this pregnancy, she's been weird about it. She keeps having these nightmares...We were in bed and I felt her body was boiling hot. She was screaming "no, no, no" in her sleep. Her breathing was heavy, tossing, and turning. It was like she was trying to get away from something. She just jolted up, dazed, didn't know where she was. It was just awful. I asked her what she was dreaming about. She says she can't remember. I begged her Dani. All she would say is it's probably her body going through changes because of the pregnancy, so she wanted me to hold her until she went to sleep. I did but the whole time she's shaking like a leaf."

"Brandon I really don't know what's going on with her. I thought she was acting weird too, but my parents seem to think it's just her hormones. It's like she doesn't even care. I will see what I can find out when I get back, but I'm not going to press her about it."

"Oh no, that's the last thing I want. I know ya'll are close, and if she won't tell me, she will tell you eventually. Okay, I gotta get back to her so thanks for listening, we'll talk more later."

After hanging up from my brother in law, my perception of him has totally changed. He's not the same guy as before. He does love my sister genuinely. This pregnancy has really changed him. Now, I like him again. Maybe I should treat him better. My sister is the one who doesn't like him for some reason.

It's one in the morning, Brock, William and I make it back to my bungalow. We were mimicking the native dance we just learned at the luau. That night Safari had us feeling majestic. We ate roasted pig, duck and alligator, drank strange, sweet tasting wine, and let the natives draw on our faces. I donned a tiara and a grass skirt that the men of the Safari luau gave me.

Brock and William received a great amount of attention from all the native women. They danced especially for them, moving seductively, together in rhythm, gyrating, and pumping their pelvis to the beat of the bongos. I jump up there with them shaking my pelvis to the music too. I did whatever the dancers were doing. They were rubbing their bodies against them, arousing them, so I rubbed my body against both of them. I stood over and straddled William's body, so far, he could see up and thru my grass skirt. Then I slowly lowered by pelvis on his pelvis grinding against him letting him know I was ready for him. The dancers whispered enchanted words in their ears, so I whispered, "fuck me" in William's ear.

Brock's a different story. I backed up into his bulging genitals grinding my ass against him, dropped it like it was hot. I turned around and rubbed my hand aggressively over his crotch, pressed my breast against his chest, and stuck my tongue in his mouth. He was ready for me. I left his embrace and continued doing what the others were doing.

The Safari was over, but we were still riding the erotic wave until we get to my hot ass room. The central air still had not been fixed which meant it was hot all over the resort. I call room service to order champagne and to make sure it's safe to get in the Jacuzzi.

"It's on!!"

I set the mood in the bungalow while the guys strip down to their underpants. William sports a boxer brief while Brock has on silk boxers.

When I lit all the candles in the room and turn the jazz station on, we are all ready to get in the Jacuzzi. The men get in with their underwear on. I take everything off. They take theirs off after I get in. We can see the stars so clearly, but I'm the only one looking at them. I'm so caught up in the mood

I forgot about the champagne, room service is at the door.

"Go get the door Billy," Brock requests quickly.

"Nope, you go get it!"

"C'mon man, you know I would but the water got my shit all..." Brock is explaining.

"Mine too man," William agrees.

"Boys, let mama handle it. Just wait here."

I stand up dripping wet, buck naked in all my glory. I see William biting his lip. Brock's eyes seem bigger than his head. They watch me walk to the door. My caramel skin glistens as the light from the stars dance over my body. I didn't bother with a towel. I answer the door, take the bottles, and bid the serviceman a goodnight. He gives me a bowl of grapes.

When I return to the veranda both men clap and whistle. Receiving the admiration, I curtsey for my two suitors. Handing the bottles to men, I set the grapes on the table and turn the music up.

Stepping down in the water, I move slowly making soft waves. Both men sit back and watch me in my nakedness move between the shadows of light. I know I look good to both of these men, and I can have either one. I just don't know which one. But the way things are going I guess I'll do them both. I sit between my new best friends.

Brock asks me to lean my head back and open my mouth. He starts pouring the champagne slowly in my mouth. It trickles down my neck. William is on the other side kissing and licking the fluid from my chin. Brock pours more of the bubbly over my breasts. William's tongue explores me softly and thoroughly, nibbling. He cups my breasts, gently squeezing the nipples between his fingers. They can feel my body responding to both of them. We agree to move to the bed.

I notice neither man is shy when coming out of the water. They've done this before. I try to check out the "packages" but the room is dark. William brought back the champagne and grapes. Brock carries me over his shoulder to the bed. His dreads were dripping wet. He lays me down as if I were a delicate bouquet of flowers meant for a most grand occasion. William turns the TV on and mutes the sound.

"Man, what are you 'bout to do watch the game?"

"Hell naw! It's too dark. I like to see what I'm eatin'," They both look at me lying there.

"What's all the chitchat about? Ya'll just gonna stand there and compare dicks?"

"Oh, hell naw!"

William grabs my foot. Brock eases his finger under my chin and they both start tickling. They watch my body quiver and jiggle with laughter.

Brock plants a barrage of kisses that lead to a deep penetrating kiss halting my schoolgirl giggling. Hot passion surges through my body piercing my inner crevice. Gently squeezing my ample breast, Brock could feel my temperature rising explosively high.

William sucks on my freshly manicured toes, massaging both my legs as he spreads them apart. He bit the right calf with just enough pain, while massaging my inner thigh relaxing my entire body.

Brock positions my arms above my head, pours champagne over and between my breasts. I can feel his warm mouth on my nipple. First the right, then the left, pulling playfully, sucking, and kissing my body.

My moaning is somewhat loud. I can't help it. It felt incredible. Experiencing this much pleasure at one time is indescribable; watching everything, every stroke of the tongues. William kisses his way to the center of my core spreading my legs wide.

I can't believe I had two men pleasuring me at the same time. I rise up so I can watch and that's when I see her.

Focusing on the door, I can see Mrs. Cheryl standing there watching everything that's going on. I didn't care. I'm feeling like a well kept sex kitten, and my kitty cat is purring making my body shake in thunderous waves.

"Oh please," I whisper.

He licks me again slowly, making me shift my hips to feel his tongue.

Mrs. Cheryl opens her mouth as she watches William French kissing my deep black triangle. I can tell she wishes it was her licking her favorite dessert.

William plunges his tongue deep then steady as if I were ice cream running down his arm.

"Do you like that baby?" Brock whispers in my ear.

"Oh yes, I do. I do."

I try to subdue my moaning but I can't. My pelvis is moving to William's tongue rhythm. I can still see Cheryl watching, licking her lips slowly. It sends my entire body into a spastic frenzy.

"Oh yes, Oh yes... I like...that's it. That's it...Oh shiiiitttt!"

Brock burst a grape in my mouth and another surge of erotic pleasure rush over my body again. We shift positions. I'm on the edge of the bed, bent over on my hands and knees. I make sure I can see my "Peeping Cheryl." She is still watching. The men are so caught up in the sexfest they never see her.

Brock is standing behind me waiting for me to back into his eager erect pole. I'm definitely not having sex without a condom this time, so I place it in my mouth just right, knelt down face to face with the lengthy rod. Both men and Cheryl watch me intently.

I put the condom on the tip and roll it onto his hardness with only my mouth.

"Damn! You know tricks too!" Brock is ready.

I assume my position.

Slowly, Brock eases into me, sending him into an ebullience of sexual desire.

"Shit girl!! What you know 'bout tooting' that ass up!" Brock teases and strokes me hard and deep.

"Like that daddy?" I ask and take in all of what Brock has to offer.

"Don't do it like that...Girl! Oooh girl!! You know you ain't right!"

I like to hear him talk to me. He's funny as fuck. I back my creamy wetness onto him slow and deep, thrusting my hips against his lower hairy v-lined abdomen, invoking my Kegel exercises. All that funny shit was replaced with moans and expressions of "shit" and "damn".

"Oh shit woman, I think..."

Before Brock finishes his sexual proclamation, his salacious juices erupt forcefully, making his body stiff with excitement and release.

After all tha,t I need a bathroom break. I

want to see what Mrs. Cheryl is up to now. When I open the door, she and I are standing face-to-face. She's nervous. I can tell, so I step closer to her. "What's up? You like what you see?"

Cheryl didn't say anything.

"I know you saw me..."

In mid-sentence, she kisses me softly using her tongue testing my response. She sat on the bathroom sink and wrapped her legs around me pulling me into her. She looks deep into my eyes, her warm hands caress my breast, and her legs spread wider. I massage her Brazilian waxed wetness with my fingers slowly right in the spot she likes.

"Hey what's going on?" William knocks on the locked door.

"I was just getting in the shower. Would you both like to join me?"

"Yeah sure."

All activity stops. Cheryl kisses me once more before leaving the bathroom quietly. I unlocked the door to find sexy ass William standing in the doorway dangling baby. Thanks to my girl, I'm ready for round two.

Nadine and I are getting off to a slow start this Monday morning. We are preoccupied in the conversation at hand. Nadine is giving an account of her last evening's events. She and her children have moved in with Calvin. She now has romantic love stories to tell.

The beginning tales of their new relationship is all she talks about. Everything is wonderful according to her. He has already sent flowers to the shop and comes to pick her up everyday for lunch. Calvin suggests she go back and finish college. Whatever she wants to do, if she wants to continue beyond her associates degree, he will pay for it. Nadine is three classes short of her associate's in social work.

"So, Calvin takes the boys to the museum while you spent the day at the salon?" I'm making sure I get all the information correct. I have to tell the story accurately to Sakoya and Stephani.

"Yes!! Can you believe that? He pays for my hair, nails, and pedicures; buys my feminine products," Nadine is bubbly feeling like a princess.

The store bell rings. We are still engrossed in the kindness of Calvin.

"Dani, when I came home, there was a beautiful peach evening gown; all accessories, purse, and shoes. He even had the right shade of pantyhose for me. Now sweetie you know that is some hard stuff to do."

"Aaaaww, that's so sweet!!"

I love listening to her stories. They were much better than her past accounts. Best of all, I didn't have to drive to the hospital to hear them.

"Where did ya'll go?"

"To the Fireman's Ball. One of Calvin's

childhood friends is a fireman. He always gives Calvin two free tickets. I'll tell you the rest later...Here comes your shadow," Nadine left me standing in the middle of the store.

"Didn't you hear me calling you?" Mrs. Cheryl is talking to me again.

"No, I'm sorry. I'll get back to work."

"Before you do that...Could you come to my office please?" Mrs. Cheryl walks away before I can answer.

"Oh, here we go."

Rolling my eyes, I reluctantly follow my boss. I already know what she wants, nothin. My boss is letting her private emotions take over at work. Something she said she could handle. Every since our sexcapade five months ago, Mrs. Cheryl has changed dramatically. Her main focus is me. She calls more than usual, gets upset when I don't return her calls, upset because she cannot control her feelings, and I on the other hand, only show professionalism at work.

Nadine, Mrs. B., and Anthony watch me as I follow the boss again. I look at their faces and know they're out there talking about it. I was so embarrassed when Nadine told me they thought we were acting strange after the convention. She said everyone was talking about how one minute Mrs. Cheryl and I could be laughing and joking one minute, and the next, she will be in her office crying for no apparent reason.

The rumor is, we got into a big argument at the convention. Mrs. B. heard Mrs. Cheryl is jealous of me because I took the guy she wanted. She also heard Mrs. Cheryl is jealous because I had more fun than she did.

Nadine wasn't listening to Mrs. B. She told

them just what I'd told her.

"No. Mrs. B. that's not true. Both of them said they had a wonderful time. Dani said they went to all the classes except for one. Then they partied the rest of the time. They did meet two guys, William and another guy."

Nadine warned me that stupid ass Anthony is going around saying he thinks we got freaky and now we don't know how to act. Nobody is listening to him.

In the office...

"Why are you always calling me back here?" I'm pissed.

"I just want to talk to you. What's wrong with that?" She's looking at me like I'm the one who is crazy, "Please have a seat."

I sit in front of the desk. Mrs. Cheryl is sitting at the edge.

"Dani what happened to all the fun we used to have? What has gotten into you? Lately, you've been acting strange as if I've done something to you," She waits for a response. I don't give one.

"Anyway, I'm wondering if you are free on Friday the... There is..."

"No, I won't be available."

Mrs. Cheryl's stood to her feet whispering loudly, "See, is all that called for? You didn't give me a chance to finish! You are so full of yourself. Thinking all I want is to be with you. It was me who listened to your sob stories over and over when Frederick dumped your ass! Remember the night you wrecked your car? Who came and picked your cryin' ass up? Me! Had your car fixed the same day? Me! It seems you have forgotten about all that, huh?"

She is standing over me in a rage. Silent,

with the I-don't-give-a-fuck-about- you- or- people- who-look-like-you look plastered on my face, Mrs. Cheryl takes her place behind the desk. She straightens her clothes and gathers her composure.

I feel drunk with power. I know exactly how my boss is feeling right now. Watching her try to remain calm, fighting feelings she has no control over. She always told me how she felt after having too much to drink.

One night after a day at Serenity Gardens, Mrs. Cheryl admitted to loving watching me with Brock and William. How it turned her on in a way she couldn't explain. She told me what she was doing to herself in the bathroom. How every dream is filled with images of me wishing William never interrupted us in the bathroom.

She revealed her feelings again when we were closing the shop last week. Mrs. Cheryl had been sipping on her "special coffee" all-day. By closing time, boss lady was feeling no pain. We stayed later than usual waiting for the exterminator to finish his job.

He left, and we were still in the office laughing just kicking it. I checked the store and locked everything. She waited by the alarm until came back.

As I set the alarm, Mrs. Cheryl tries to kiss me and feel on my breast.

"Kiss me, *please!*" She begged me. I can remember the look of desperation on her face. I snap out of my trance.

"Is that all? May I go back to work now?"

"Yes, that is all... Oh, will you be able to work Saturday?" She tries to lighten the mood.

"No, I promised my father I would work at his shop Saturday. I haven't been there lately," I walk out of the office. I can't wait 'til this day is over.

I rock Manasha to sleep and put her in her bed because in the middle of the night she will come creeping in my bed with three of her dolls.

I start moving furniture and cleaning up my new spacious apartment. I found a better spot for my hand painted portrait of myself. It will be the first thing everyone sees when they visit.

I made a call to my sister to make sure she was ok. The baby could come at any moment; I am ready.

Everyone was so happy when Stephani told the family she was pregnant. Now the time has finally come. Although her pregnancy has taken a toll on her, she was high risk from the beginning due to emotional stress. The doctor said, because Stephani has wanted to have this baby for so long, she has stressed herself worrying.

I think there is something more going on. I can't put my finger on it, but I know there is something else wrong. Stephani has always taken care of her body. She is not a worrying person.

All through her pregnancy, there's been nothing but trauma. The doctor sedated Stephani twice for hallucinations. She'd wake up in the middle of the night screaming. I witnessed one of her episodes while I was staying at her house. The doctor also prescribed medicine for Stephani to sleep.

She was afraid of the darkness because something would always terrify in her dreams. All the lights stayed on in the house until she went to sleep. Stephani cried all the time for no reason. When she was able to get out of bed, she was a wreck. She didn't comb her hair; jittery all the time.

I knew there was a problem when Manasha asked in the saddest voice, "Mommy where is Aunt Stevie?"

Not only had Manasha spent the night, Stephani was sitting right in front of her.

"Is something in your eye, baby? You see Stephani right there," I checked her eyes.

"Not my Aunt Stevie," Manasha left the room in search of Constance.

The doctor insists it's stress and nothing more.

My cell phone is ringing.

"Hello?" The voice on the other end started laughing.

"Hey, girl! What's up! I'm on my way over to check you out."

"Where are you?"

"I'm right around the corner. I picked us up a little something. See you in a minute."

Sakoya walks into my townhouse apartment with her mouth gaped open.

"Congratulations!!" She gives me a hug as she steps into my spacious new apartment.

"This is so comfy!! Oh... Dani, first please let me say I'm sorry for not helping you move, but Quinton was in town. Plus... You called me at the last minute. You have everything organized anyway. You didn't need me. Plus...I been working all that overtime," Sakoya ran out of excuses.

"Do you remember Regina's friend's cousin Michelle?" Sakoya asks while she looks around, "Do you have central air?" She asked another question before I can answer the first.

"No. I don't know Michelle. Yes, I have central air. Can't you feel it?"

"She lives in the next complex over, but hers is not decked out like this. Who helped you?"

"My parents! No thanks to you! It's cool though. Mom is happy for me and 'Nasha. She told me she was proud but I needed to come back to church. I told her I was coming."

"What did your dad say?" Sakoya likes to know everything.

"Well, he told me to pay my bills on time. Always lock both locks. Keep a flashlight and a bat by your headboard," We cracked up to my fathers' anecdotes.

"Who painted this picture of you?" Sakoya is looking closely at the signature.

"A friend of mine, back in July, I think," She's so nosey.

"Whoever painted this is the bomb. How many hours did you have to sit there like that? Or did you take a picture like that and then gave it to them?

"I gave him a picture, damn! Can we get on with the tour?"

Escorting my first visitor around my two-story townhouse, I am proud. Proud of my accomplishment, I set my mind to do something and I did it. Not only that, although my best friend is happy for me, she's still a tad jealous. I love it! We visit each room. I share my plans for each one. We stop in Manasha's room.

"Well, how's your sister? She ready to go yet? I know she can't wait to drop that load. Plus it's hot! Too hot to be toting a baby in ya belly."

"No, she isn't ready to go. She says she isn't ready to be a mother. She wants to give the baby up for adoption."

"What? What is wrong with her? What does Brandon say about all this? I know he's trippin'. I wonder what brought all this on?"

"I couldn't tell you. It's scaring my parents, Brandon even Constance has said something to me. This is not just the "baby blues.""

"My parents keep to themselves, but they are terribly worried asking me all kinds of questions. I don't know what to tell them. We don't want to upset Stephani at all. You know mom has a way... I'm just going to wait until the baby gets here. Then I'll see if she changes at all or if she gets worse. Right now Brandon is taking care of her. He has taken a leave of absence just to take care of her. He hasn't had a vacation in three years. I thought maybe he wouldn't because he just got that position..."

"What position?" Sakoya interrupted.

"He is the Vice President of FloTu Industries."

"Girl, shut yo mouth!! That is wonderful. But damn now his wife is all messed up."

"Well that's what I don't understand. When I was staying there, I remember him leaving for his last meeting right before he became vice president. I distinctly remember Stephani's enthusiasm because he told her things were going to change. He said he was ready to have a family. So all this other talk... I just don't get it. Anyway, so where's my apartment-warming gift?" I change the subject to lighten the mood.

I had already bought us a bottle of wine to drink while we unpack the rest of my things. I have to fill her in on the latest gossip. Sakoya hands me another bottle of wine as my apartment warming gift. Great minds think alike.

"She had you in the office just to ask could you work Saturday?"

"No, she was trying to get me to go somewhere with her Friday," Correcting Sakoya again.

"Friday, this is Friday?"

"I don't know. I didn't give her a chance to finish telling me."

"Girl, she just wanted to be alone with you. I told you! She is too, too sweet to you. She didn't buy me nothing!" Sakoya rolls her eyes while taking a sip.

"I knew she was up to something. She was buying all kinds of crap for you. People don't do craziness like that unless they want something." Sakoya keeps on with her rant.

"She is a good friend. It's just now everything has changed. Before, when we were hanging out, it was cool. Now, all she wants to do is "continue what we started.""

"Girl, she wants you bad! You done turned the girl out. What about her husband? Oh, that's right he's in a wheelchair. Aaawww, poor lady she ain't gettin' none as it is. Now you treating her like shit," Sakoya stops unpacking and pours herself another.

"Whatever! I haven't done anything to that woman. She is just tripping 'cause she saw some big girl pimpin' and now she wants a sample!!"

Sakoya almost choked from laughing so hard at me.

I trust Sakoya with everything, but she has no idea what really happened in the bungalow. I told her Mrs. Cheryl saw Brock, William, and me in the bed together and now she wants me.

"Have you talked to that guy anymore? You know the one that comes in the card store and the hardware store. What's his name again?"Sakoya starts the next barrage of questions.

"Christian Mitchell. Yes, he was in the store the same day that heffa had me in her office. Nadine told me he came in as soon as I went to the back. She said he looked like he was looking for me."

My cell phone rings, after checking the number, "It's her, girl." We laugh. I let it ring.

"Well, did you get to talk to Christian?" Sakoya wants all the details.

"Well, for a minute. He likes to be called Chris. Each time he comes in we always speak. He finally admitted the clamp I suggested worked better."

"You told me that. I think that was the third time you saw him. That's all, that's it?"

"So, anyway, I asked him who he buys the get well cards for every Friday. He told me his mother. She has cancer, and loves reading the cards. She keeps all of them. That's why it takes him so long to find one because it has to say pretty close to how he's feeling.

He has his own construction company, 28 years old, three brothers, and a dog, Buster. He lives at home with his mom right now, so he can keep an eye on her."

"Good job, hell great job 'cause he don't have to answer to nobody but himself. You said he was fine, right? Plus he takes care of his mother. If a man takes care of his mother, you know he'll take care of you."

I admire him for that.

"Didn't you say, your father told you he

asked about you in the hardware store?" sakoya asks.

"Yep. He came back to the store asking who I was."

"He told me he made the guy tell him something about himself before he was able to talk to his daughter."

"No he didn't!" Sakoya is grinning.

"Yes girl. He's originally from Florida and moved here when he was sixteen. He lived with his father then moved here with his mom. His parents divorced when he was ten. He and his younger brother chose to live with his father. His mother left and moved here to be close to her mother. She passed away a year and a half ago.

He didn't do too much until he met me because he pretty much never left her side. He thinks something will happen when he's not around. She found out she had cancer last summer."

"Your father got the four, one, one. He must have been in that store for a good hour. Good detective work. Your daddy don't play when it comes to his girls, does he?" We burst into laughter again.

"I thought you said he had three brothers."

"Well, I don't have every detail yet but I'm working on it. My father wants me to go out with him. He has asked me out... but I'm not ready yet. I've been having a great time enjoying myself. Oh, did I tell you Brock and William called me," I sashayed into the kitchen to refresh both glasses and opened another bottle.

"You late-night-streetwalker!!"

We hi-five each other and continue our sappy yet sexy gossip session. I give my best friend all the juicy tid-bits of each call. Sakoya can't believe both men wanted to see me again, separately. I told her about the date I had with the exterminator I met at the store. The time lapsed until the wee hours in the morning. We were still laughing comparing stories, and reminiscing about school days. How Manasha is growing up so fast. I show Sakoya the latest picture of Manasha eating an ice-cream cone with her Papa.

I fill her in on my sister's progress or should I say regression. It's all getting to be too much for all of us because we can't help; we don't know what's wrong

My cell phone rings again. It's one forty-five in the morning. I haven't seen this number before. I know it's Mrs. Cheryl calling from another line so I will answer.

"I know this is her again," I let it ring.

"Well, I think you should go out with the Chris guy too. He sounds like a well-rounded guy."

Sakoya wants me to get back in the dating game, but I'm fine. Right now, I need to slow it down for myself. I just came off a whirlwind of hot loveless sex not too long ago with three very different people. It was all good, truly the best, but I know there is more to life than that. I know eventually I'm going to want someone special. It will be around the next holiday. That's when I really want someone so I can get a gift or something; do something romantic or just unforgettable; create memories. I do think of things like that from time to time.

"You have to be careful about those kinda guys. They are the ones you don't suspect. Anyway, I'm good. I like being single running things my way! No more bullshit to deal with none of that. Trust me. I sleeps well at night," I had to let her know.

"Yeah, but you can't judge Chris by what Frederick did. You'll never find love doing that."

"Frederick? Girl bye! I am not still on that! I learned my lesson. He taught me well! That's all I gotta say about that. Anyway, what's been happening with you?" I'm ready to hear what her life is all about.

Sakoya goes on to tell me she is on a quest of self-discovery. That's where all that talk came from. How she is waiting for the right man and not chasing just any man. No more meaningless sex for her. She's ready to take true responsibilities for her actions. Sakoya is ready to settle down and have some kids, blah, blah, blah.

"You having a dry spell?"

"Yep."

My cell phone rings again.

"That's Mrs. Cheryl stalkin' you," Sakoya starts laughing.

I check the number. It's definitely not Cheryl, but I need to leave for about an hour.

"Hey, since you celibate right now, will you stay here for a minute? I just remembered I gotta go to the store," I start putting on my shoes.

"Being celibate works! Sell a bit and then give a little bit away, so when you and Chris finally get it on, make him buy you something for your services.

"Shut up! That's crazy! Be right back."

Sakoya agrees to stay quickly, but I know why, she spotted my closets upstairs and wants to go through them. She's not fooling me.

Another Sunday morning, and I'm up fixing Manasha's oatmeal. She's waiting impatiently for her food.

"Peeze mommy, eat!"

I set the bowl in front of her and went into the kitchen. My mind drifts to the happenings at the church. I miss going, but not ready to go back and face all the members. Although I've seen many of the saints at the store, they all ask when I'm coming back. I can't face Rev. Booker. When I look at him, I know I will just die. He will look at me differently. I won't be the innocent girl he believed me to be. Flashing back to how awful I acted on that Sunday, I still cringe wishing I could take it all back.

Then Frederick's face appears in my mind, the pain, and hurt returns as if it happened yesterday.

The phone rings. It's Stephani.

"Hey girl. How ya feeling?"

"I'm doing o.k. I guess. Where's 'Nasha?"

"She's here eating. Did you go to your doctor's appointment Friday?"

"Yeah we went. Brandon is getting on my nerves. He's always asking all these extra questions just pissing me off! The doctor gives me an ultrasound, so we looking at the baby on the screen, right? He has the nerve to say the baby got his profile! He actually turns his head to the side trying to show his profile. See, that's just stupid."

"He's a proud father that's all. He just wants you and the baby to be all right. You can't be mad at that. Stephani tell me what's wrong."

"Why does everyone keep asking me that? I don't know!" Stephani is yelling at me.

"Ok, Ok, me and 'Nasha are on our way over."

"Ok."

Once we get there, we retreat to the den to talk. My sister is calm like nothing ever happened on the phone. She is talking about everything but what is bothering her. We talk about how we both miss going to church. Stephani urges me to go back, and I urge her to tell me what's going on with her.

"Everybody falls short of the glory, so there is no reason you shouldn't go back. You know it would make mom and dad happy to see you."

"I know but... It's so scary. Every body looking at me like I'm crazy and whispering behind my back. I don't know if I can handle all of that; all the questions. You know somebody is going to tell me all about Frederick and Chloe. I don't want to hear none of it. Then on top of that, I have to talk to Rev. Booker and give an apology to the entire congregation. I think I'm going to wait a little while longer."

"I think the sooner you go the better you'll feel," Stephani reminds me again.

"Why didn't you go to church with Brandon today?" I quiz her.

"Well, last night I went to the emergency room..."

"Emergency room! Why didn't you call me?"

"Let me finish please! The doctor said I was starting to have those Braxton Hicks contractions or something like that. I did call. You didn't answer your cell. It was about one forty in the morning. Where were you?"

"I was at home. I guess I didn't hear the

phone," I didn't want to tell her the real reason why I didn't answer the phone.

"Well, I thought you were breaking in your new apartment, under some man, tramp!" My sister is laughing. Something she hasn't done in a longtime.

"Yeah, real cute. I'm a let you get away with that 'cause you're with child, but once you drop that waterhead..."

In an instant Stephani's laughter turns to blubbering tears, I sent Manasha out of the room to get a snack from Constance. I don't ask any questions. I just hold her and tell her everything will work itself out.

"This is strange. It's usually you comforting me. *Whatever* it is, I promise, it will be all right. That's what you always tell me."

This is why *Claw-deeen* and daddy had us going to church," I like pronouncing mama's name like that it always makes Stephani smile, "So when crap like...*Whatever* it is you're going through you'll know that Jesus will fix it. I know you've already prayed about it. Now leave it alone. *Whatever* it is, leave it alone. Let *Him* handle it. You've done all you can do. You can't let this eat you up. That's exactly what you've done, worried yourself sick but won't let us help.

As much as I hate to admit it, Brandon is doing a great job. He just wanted to stay focused on that promotion. Once he got what he wanted...Excuse me, deserved, his focus is now on you and the baby. That's what you wanted. Now *you* have flipped the script. Why?"

I give my sister a big squeeze and rub on her belly. It shifts when I put my hand on her stomach.

We laugh, cry, and hug for as long as we can

stand it. I feel a little like our mother.

Stephani is ready to reveal what's been bothering her. She turns to me, and the tears start to roll again. She wiped her face clean then took a deep breath.

"Mommy, mommy nook. I got cooo-kies!" Manasha runs into the room interrupting the explanation.

"Yes baby. That's wonderful," I'm not paying any attention to my baby girl. My eyes are tearing quickly watching Stephani struggle for words.

"Mommy… mommy! MOMMEEEE!"

Manasha is screaming at me with cookie remnants around her mouth, on her hands, and in her hair. Immediately, I walk the toddler to the TV in the other room and put in her favorite video.

When I return, Stephani's was kneeling by the couch. She is breathing heavily and starting to sweat.

"My contractions have started. Call Brandon on his cell."

Stephani directs in a normal voice and rose to her feet. After the contraction, she moves slowly to get her belongings for the hospital stay. I'm following closely behind. Constance is making sandwiches.

Checking the nursery Brandon designed and decorated himself, she leaves the night-light on for the baby's return. Started her shower water and closed the bathroom door in my face.

"Yes! Yes! Her water broke! She's has her overnight bag at the door and she's taking a shower now. Yes a shower! Ok…Ok I'll just take her in my car, and we'll meet you at the hospital."

I called our parents, and Sakoya repeated the

same information. They all agreed to meet at the hospital.

"The doctor sent her back home and told us to wait until she dilated five centimeters. That was two days ago!" I'm explaining to Nadine as we are stocking shelves at work.

"Wow, it wasn't that long ago I had my Gabbs. Yep, she probably wants to clean the entire house. That's called the nesting stage. I learned that on cable."

Mrs. Cheryl is in the shop, straightening displays, and watering the plants. She moves about the store swiftly. Cleaning and dusting as she rearranged the cards and envelopes. We overhear her warning Anthony about talking to all the women customers. We knew he meant no harm, and he just doesn't know any better.

Anthony with his toothpick hanging from his mouth escorts Mrs. Fugate across the street. She's a regular customer. She gives him a kiss on the cheek after he opens her car door. He holds the door open and waits for the large breasted young woman to get in. We can see she let her window down, then all of a sudden, she speeds out of the parking lot. Anthony rushes back to the shop.

"You never learn do you?"

He gives me the finger then proceeds to help the bosslady hang a sign in the window for the play, The Wiz. Everyone in the store is starting to ask questions.

"Are the tickets on sale now?"

"No, we start selling them tomorrow."

"What day is it?"

"Friday the twenty-fifth."

"That's this weekend!"

"There is only going to be one showing."

It is time for my break, but I stay out front to hear the details of the play. I want to know about backstage passes so I can meet the cast members.

The Wiz is my favorite play, I remember my parents taking me and Stephani when we were young. Afterwards, we went out to eat. It was a magical night. I was also cast as the good witch in my sixth grade rendition.

Mrs. Cheryl went to finish her paperwork. Nadine and I are still reviewing the play information.

"Can I get some assistance?" Chris is standing in front of the register.

Nadine leaves us alone. She went to the front of the store so she could see everything.

"Hello, Christian. What brings you here on a Wednesday?" My flirt mode just turns on.

"I came to see you."

"Oh, that's a good answer. Let me get someone to cover the register."

Nadine came to the register before I called her. We step outside for a little privacy.

"I want to know are you seeing anyone."

That question caught me off guard. I wasn't expecting that so I didn't really have an answer.

"I thought you were because you declined my offer to go have a drink, but your father told me you weren't seeing anyone. So what's up?"

"My father said what?"

"Yeah, he told me a few details about his little *peanut*."

I am shocked at this point. My father didn't tell me he told him that.

"See, that's why you should go out with me to find out what your daddy is saying about his precious peanut."

His offer sounds so inviting but I'm not ready. Oh, but he's so fine! I'm enjoying my freedom. If I say yes to his proposal I know it will end in disaster. He looks like he could put down in the sack though! He would be my rebound man. I'm just out for fun, no strings. I can look at him and tell he's never been any woman's rebound man. I would fall head over hills in stupid love with him then I'd be in the same predicament as before, nope can't do it! Another Frederick incident is too much for me to handle right now.

"Look, I don't know what my father told you, but I can't go out with you. I have plans, and I don't need your kind of disruption right now! Please don't call me peanut."

"Disruption! So I'm a disruption? Do I disrupt you?" Chris is being sarcastic and silly.

"No, I didn't say all that..."

Mrs. Cheryl makes a point to step outside to tell me break is over. She gives Chris the once over and went back into the store.

"Think about it, and if you want to go, let me know. Don't make me go back to your father's store and tell on you, *peanut.*"

Mixed in the mail is an envelope with Danielle typed on the front. I thought that was odd because no one uses my first name. Inside the envelope, is a ticket and backstage pass to The Wiz. I jump up and down screaming in my new apartment.

I call my sister to thank her for the ticket. I figured she got it for me since I talked about it all day.

Stephani has no idea what I'm talking about. She is excited for me and wishes she could go but the baby is due anytime now. I offer to stay with her instead of going but she insists I go. She is sure the baby isn't ready to come yet.

Pulling into the parking lot, early the next morning, I realize the ticket is from Mrs. Cheryl.

"Dammit! Dammit! Dammit!" I literally threw a fit in my car. She will stop at nothing to get my attention. I wish I hadn't led her on and played with her emotions. I had no idea such a fine lady could act like this. I've made it perfectly clear I don't have the same feelings she has for me. At this very moment, I feel like a Frederick!

I want to go to the play desperately, but if means shielding off Mrs. Cheryl's advances all night, then I'll wait until the play comes around again.

Something tells me Mrs. Cheryl is up to something. I decide to give the ticket back. As much as I really want to go, I can't lead Mrs. Cheryl on anymore. I will simply decline her offer and tell her flat out it's over. I would like to remain friends but I know it's not possible.

With ticket in hand, I march into Mrs. Cheryl's office. I start my speech I rehearsed in the car.

"Thank you for thinking of me, but I can't accept this," I laid the ticket on her desk and continued, "We have shared a lot in the past, and I thank you for every opportunity you've given me. Cheryl, you've taught me more than you can imagine, but we cannot be together. I don't know what happened to our friendship...Well, I know what happened, but we cannot continue to be friends if you keep acting this way. I'm sorry."

"First off, it's *Mrs.* Cheryl thank you. What are you talking about?"

I picked up the ticket. Showed her the

center isle, floor seat with the exclusive backstage pass.

"You just came in here showing off. I already have my tickets for the VIP section, *Miss sorry*! Close the door on your way out," Sipping her coffee she turns a page in the newspaper.

I'm confused, asking everyone at work and home no one knew about the ticket. I rack my brain all-day while tearing my closet apart for something to wear.

Nothing, I found absolutely nothing to wear, so I call my big sis. I need to check on her condition, as well as use her charge card. Everything is still the same although she sounds as if she's been crying again. At this moment, I realize we never finish our discussion. Before I got a chance to ask her about the conversation, Brandon picks up the receiver and asks me to spend the night. He explains he has a meeting he can't miss, but he doesn't want his wife home alone.

"Sure bro-in-law, but I do have a fee..."
Arriving at my sister's in the outfit she bought, I am promptly greeted with, "Where are you going? I thought you were spending the night tonight?"
Brandon is checking out my gear.

"I am as soon as the play is over. I'll be here. I got a replacement until I get back." I had to reassure him because he's looking at me like I've lost my mind.

"Who?"

"Just keep your phone on. I got a feeling the baby will come tonight." I'm laughing at myself because once they see who is standing in for me...

"Hi Uncle Brandon!" he knew that little voice anywhere.

"Hey Badness" he gives her a quick spin, kisses Stephani on her forehead, and attempts to leave.

"Hello son, you in a rush? Don't you think you should stay home? Stephani is real close to having this baby. You're going to miss it."

Our mother is standing in his doorway. She continues with her advice, "Stop calling her badness...That's why she acts so badly."

"Hello, yes mother I am in a rush. I cannot stay home but my cell phone is on. As soon as you all leave for the hospital call me, I'll be on my way back. I will try to be here before the baby gets here. I have to go."

Brandon runs to give his wife a kiss. He's out the door quickly. He gives me the evil eye behind his mother-in-laws back.

"Momma, I'm leaving too. All of the phone numbers are on the refrigerator. Call me only if she is ready to go, and I'll meet ya'll at the hospital."

"She won't go before you get back," mom says.

"Oh, I think she will."

Mrs. Claudine walks into the den where her eldest daughter has set up camp writing a letter. Everything is at her disposal. What she doesn't have Constance will surely fetch it.

I peek in the room to see my sister's face. She has no idea our faultfinding mother will be staying with her until I come back from the play. I blew kisses teasingly and left. Stephani tries to get up but Mrs. Claudine warns her oldest child, "You need to sit down and rest yourself. This is the time to prepare for the delivery. What are you going to name the child? Are you still having them nightmares? What are you writing?"

Miss Kim

I can hear mama interrogating Stephani on my way out the door. I have to laugh because I know she wants to kill me right about now.

The usher shows me to my seat. I'm excited, but I never found out who sent me the ticket. I'm a few minutes early. No one sits to the right or left of me. I go to the bathroom. Maybe when I get back there will be someone sitting there, like a surprise. There were many couples and families in attendance. I'm feeling a little out of place because I'm here at my favorite play, alone. These are the times I feel the worst, especially holidays.

Frederick would attend all sorts of events with me. Plays were our favorite. We would pick the play apart over dinner afterwards.

The lights flickered alerting the playgoers to get to their seats. My phone vibrates in my knock off Prada bag.

"Poor baby, had to attend the show alone my pretty!" Mrs. Cheryl mimicked the wicked witch over the phone.

"Lady! Sit down! We cannot see," I can hear the people in the background. It sounds pretty close, I hang up.

The curtain fell and the lights go out. The playhouse is quiet. The anticipation is high in the audience. The curtain rises and the dramatic voice-over begins. Dorothy is center stage.

I'm almost at the edge of my seat trying to listen to every word, when a latecomer comes down my row. All I can hear is "Please excuse me...'scuse me...I'm sorry."

I shift my body, so this huge man can sit right next to me. I can't believe... it is! It's him!

"Oh you are so sneaky!! You set this all up!" I'm whispering loudly.

"Ssshhh! Please be quiet. I can't hear,"
Chris puts his index finger up to his mouth.

I'm flattered that he went through so much
trouble for me. He must have heard me asking all
those questions the other day. Well, I have to give
it to him. He is smooth with his game. I felt all
special. I have to check myself making sure I am
not grinning too hard.

My phone vibrates again in my lap. I know
it's Cheryl letting me know she sees everything.
Now she's furious because she thinks me and Chris
are seeing each other. I check the number.

Whispering, I answer the call. It's my
mother telling me my sister is in serious pain. They
were going to take her to hospital. She already
called Brandon. He's on his way.

"Chris, I'm sorry I have to leave. My sister
is getting ready to have her baby," I whisper softly
in his ear. Chris walks me out to the vestibule. We
stand facing each other.

"Thanks for the ticket. I feel so bad. You
went through all that trouble to get the ticket, and
now I have to go to Good Samaritan."

"Well, that's all right. It was worth it to see
the expression on your face when I sat next to you.
You think I might be able to take you out for that
drink now?"

"Yeah sure, when?" My cheeks hurt from
grinning.

"How about after your sister has the baby,"
Chris is smiling too.

"What?"

"How about I ride with you to the hospital,"
He grabs my hand and we walk to my car.

"See, I had one of my dudes drop me off
here that's why I was so late."

"Why would you do that?"

"So, you would have to take me with you when you left."

"I see you real slick. I gotta keep both eyes on you!"

My phone vibrates against the steering wheel. I had it in my hand all while talking to Chris. I have to answer it so it doesn't look suspect.

"Hello?" I know Cheryl is on the other end.

"Where you go? I saw you and your boyfriend leave the theater. What's up with that? You can't wait 'til after the play! You gotta fuck him right now whore!"

"Oh, no sir. I don't want a subscription to trout mouth digest. Thank you."

Stephani is freaking out. She can't get comfortable. She wants everyone out of the room except for me. Our parents, Sakoya, Constance, and Manasha are patiently waiting in the waiting room. Brandon hasn't made it to the hospital yet.

I try opening the curtains but Stephani wants it dark. I just sit on the bed because whatever I do it's not right.

Stephani's face is so puffy and swollen from crying. Her nose is red and raw. She turns to me and says, "I don't think this is Brandon's baby! I want you to read this letter then tear it up!"

I reach for more tissue. "What? What did you say?"

Stephani tries to get the words out, but the contractions are coming harder and faster. She puts the letter in my hand.

"Brandon doesn't know. I don't even..." An overflow of tears muffles Stephani's words.

"Whose baby is it?"

A contraction starts. I'm breathing and panting along with Stephani until it subsides. I ring the buzzer for the nurse.

"I don't know... All I remember is a man in a ski mask. I woke up in my bed naked. Dani please... I don't know what to do. Brandon is going to leave me. I never told him about it. He's not going to believe me," Stephani is frantic and nervous. She has a death grip on my hand.

The nurse comes in with a calming voice.

"Hi there. Let's see if we're ready to have a baby," The nurse went to the foot of the bed to check Stephani's progress.

"Yes, I think we're ready. Are you her coach?" The nurse smiles at me.

"Yes, I am until her husband gets here."

"No! No! You can't let him in," Stephani pleads.

"You're gonna have to calm down Stephani. It will be fine. Let's get the doctor in here, but you're going to have to relax."

"Don't worry about Brandon. He's not going to leave you," I whisper in her ear. I don't want strangers to hear our conversation.

"I don't want this baby if it's not Brandon's!" The nurse and the doctor stop talking for a moment. I'm sweating.

"Stephani, we need you to concentrate on having this baby, all right?" The doctor was talking as if Stephani is in danger.

"We need to keep your blood pressure stable. You have to help us ok? Breathe... That's good." I walk away for a moment to read the letter.

The room door open. It's Brandon. He rushes to Stephani's side. He's already in his delivery clothes. I fold the letter quickly and stuff it in my bra.

Stephani takes one look at him and burst into tears. A painful contraction starts, I can tell by the way she screams directly into my ear and squeezes my hand harder. That's my cue to leave.

"No! Stay! Please," Brandon insists.

"Keep pushing...C'mon."The doctor is directingStephani

"We can see the baby's head!"The nurse announced.

I'm on Stephani's left side clutching her hand. Brandon is to the right coaching; speaking softly to his wife. I'm in awe of the whole scene.

The man in front of me is a loving and caring man. He is in love with Stephani. I remember all the times Brandon confided in me about his wife. He worried, thinking Stephani didn't love him anymore. He thought she hadn't forgiven him for making her wait to have this baby. I remember him saying he wanted to have a large family. It was the timing. He was so close to his promotion, and he didn't want to blow it.

"Push Stephani! C'mon you can do it!" Brandon puts a cool towel on Stephani's forehead and fed her ice chips.

Cries of a newborn baby fill the delivery room.

"It's a boy! Go ahead dad and cut the umbilical cord," The doctor instructs.

Brandon's eyes lit up. He wanted a boy. Taking the cutting instrument from the doctor, Brandon cuts the cord. Smiles at his wife and kisses her hand.

"I knew you could do it!"

Stephani never let go of my hand. I'm so happy for my sister right now! But when I look in her eyes, I see she is terrified. The nurse takes the baby to clean him off.

"Here's your baby boy Stephani!" The kindhearted nurse places the baby in his mother's arms. Brandon is standing proud at the head of the bed.

Stephani's eyes have a twinkle. She has to smile. He is precious. They have him wrapped like a baby mummy. Everyone piles into the delivery room.

Stephani wants to count all fingers and toes. She unwraps the warm blanket just to take a peek. The blanket falls from around the baby's head. He has a head full of coal, curly black hair. His ears are much darker than his present complexion.

"Look, his birthmark is near his eye," Brandon points out.

Stephani blacks out.

Brandon is hysterical. He demands the doctors give him an explanation.

"What the hell is going on with my wife?" He's trying to hold it together.

I can't bear to see him like this, so I felt it was time for me to step in. I know my sister will hate me for this but I don't know what to do. I can't let it get any worse. Stephani has passed out with her newborn baby in her arms! I couldn't forgive myself if something else happened and I did nothing to stop it.

I take Brandon outside the hospital and try my best to explain. I only repeat the bits and pieces I heard. Nevertheless, it isn't enough to satisfy Brandon. The only thing he hears is the baby may not be his. I give him the letter. He reads it right there.

Something happened to me the night after

my final meeting with Dr. Scott. I remember leaving his house in a hurr.y I didn't want to be there. I got home and poured myself a glass a wine downstairs in the kitchen. I remember calling you letting you know I was home. I checked the house because Brandon was on his way home the next day. I ran bathwater, the phone rang, and I answered it in the bedroom. My glass of wine was on the night stand. I don't remember bringing it upstairs. After I talked to Brandon, I drank more wine and felt dizzy. I tried to call you again but the phone line was dead!

That's when I saw him, a man dressed in all black with a ski mask on his face. I woke up the next morning lying in bed naked! I never sleep in the nude. I felt pain between my legs and had a white film on me and the sheets. He raped me.

"I knew she was fucking him! I knew it! That's why she has been acting so strange. It all makes sense now! How could she do something like that to me! Now she's saying she was raped? C'mon man! That's the cover up! You believe this shit Dani?"

I plead with him to listen with his heart and beg him to really look at the situation.

"Replay your lives together. Your wife wouldn't lie to you about something like that. Until now, you haven't had any problems. You have been blessed. Now a major problem has surfaced, this is where your faith, your trust, your belief in God comes in." I'm reminding him of a passage from one of Rev. Booker's sermons. Brandon isn't listening.

"She kept going to see the doctor when I wasn't going. That's when she started seeing him I bet."

"No, Brandon she was not. I repeat she's not having an affair."

"She was having something...She went to his house! Is she still with him? All this time she never said a word."

I try my best to help Brandon to understand, but it's going to take an act from God before he could grasp it all. He makes a call.

"Delivery ward please. Hello this is Brandon Caldwell. My wife just delivered my son. How long before he can leave the hospital? No, when can *he* leave?"

I could see the tears nestled in the bottom of Brandon's eyelids. All the frustration he has endured from the beginning of the pregnancy is taking a toll on him. He doesn't know what to do or how to feel.

"Everything will work itself out. I promise."

"How can you promise such a thing?! You don't know! This is no minor shit! My wife doesn't know who the father of her baby is! She never told me she was raped!"

I watch Brandon speed away in his brand-spankin'-new Benz.

Miss Kim

Packing the last of the sandwiches, Nadine is finally ready for a day at the beach. She, Calvin, Chris and I made plans to take all the kids, Calvin's daughter Kaitlin, Nadine's boys Robert, Nathan, the newest addition, Gabrielle, and Manasha.

I can tell new the couple has grown very fond of each other. Feeding each other and always grinning at their inside jokes. Finishing each others sentences, you know just sappy. Nadine is always smiling like she getting it on a regular basis and she is pleased. Calvin is her prince charming.

The car stops and children jump out.

"Before you leave, grab a bag or something!" Calvin's request stops the children from running off.

Nadine balances the baby on her chest while carrying the diaper bag, stroller, and play pin, she insisted.

We find a spot with just enough shade. The guys put the umbrella up and we get the sunscreen flowing. The kids drop the bags and coolers right where they stood. They looked to Calvin to see if they could make a dash for it.

"Put sunscreen on first please," Nadine makes them sit down.

"You need to stick together at all times. You guys are older so watch out for the girls and check in from time to time. Your mother and I will be right here. Stay out of trouble!" The kids are out of site before we can tell them to have a good time.

Calvin brought his portable television, so they wouldn't miss the games. We ladies, lay under the shade sipping on home made potent coladas, one of my specialties.

Two sips and Nadine told me everything about Stewart. How they started as high school sweethearts and how he was her first lover. They were crazy and wild together in their "bar hopping stage." How she vowed she would never leave him.

Stewart got a job at the paper mill while she went to community college. They moved in together and soon she was pregnant. The boys were born a year apart. He never batted an eye. Whatever she wanted to do or not do was fine with him. That's what she loved about him.

For awhile, Stewart maintained his position as supervisor at the mill, but soon his job was moving over seas. Overtime ceased, hours cut drastically, and he wasn't bringing home enough money to pay the bills. That's when Nadine started looking for work.

"You remember?"

"Yeah, I remember."

The tears roll down her cheeks. She tells me in detail how he tried to kill her on several occasions by choking her 'til she blacked out. Stewart would drink and verbally abuse her. He would just rant and rave all around the house, breaking lamps, kicking doors, scaring the Robert and Nathan. She was so scared for her boys.

Being pregnant with their third child, threw him over the edge. From that point on, he was a monster, so full of rage, and out of control. She said all he fussed about was the money. How they didn't have enough.

Stewart always blamed Nadine for his abusive behavior. Never taking responsibility for his actions it was always her fault. He said she was selfish and one-sided. Nadine repeats his words, "If you wouldn't have that baby, you wouldn't get beat."

I listen as she went on about her clients down at the shelter where she volunteers. She says they depend on her a great deal. Fridays are usually pretty busy days for her, a chess rematch with Mrs. Upland, bingo in the gymnasium. She hoped someone named Marlene remembers to get Caroline to sign her release papers. Nadine cancelled her lecture on the beginning signs of abuse to come to the beach.

Today is a wonderful day to be at the beach. The sky is clear, sun is hot and the water is right. We play in the sand with the babies while Calvin and Chris walk over to the bar. It seems they want something a little stronger than the daiquiris I made. I think they don't want to hold the decorative fruity glasses I brought for the occasion.

"Look mom!!!" The boys jumped around.

"Look who we found on the other side of the beach!!"

Nadine removes her sunglasses and stands to her feet. She looks around to see Chris, Calvin, and Kaitlin slowly approaching the area

"Hello, Nadine."

"Hello, Stewart," Nadine grabs her beach towel and wraps it around her waist like a skirt.

"I don't want to cause any problems. The boys begged me to come over here," Stewart turns his attention to the lady next to him, "Aahh, this is my wife Rebecca. We just wanted to..." Stewart's words were fading away. He can't look Nadine in her eyes.

"Hi you doing? I've heard so much about you and your boys," Rebecca shakes Nadine's hand briefly, "Stewart wanted to come over here and ask if he could come and visit with the boys sometimes.

He sure misses them a great deal. It would mean so much to him, to us."

The boys, Stewart, and his wife Rebecca are all staring at Nadine waiting for a response.

Chris joins me, Manasha, and Gabrielle just a few feet away.

"Stewart, Rebecca, this is my... This is, Calvin and his daughter Kaitlin," Kaitlin jumps down off her father and joins us.

"Hey guess what?" Chris is trying to get my attention. I was keeping a careful eye on the drama unfolding right in front of me.

"Calvin is going to ask Nadine to marry him."

"What? When? Really? When?"

"Before you spoil the surprise, please keep your mouth shut and act natural," Chris is talking to me as if I was ten.

"He is trying to figure out when. He wants it to be special."

Everyone exchanges pleasantries again. Nadine excuses herself and Calvin from the group. She takes him to the side to talk to him privately but her boys are following them too.

"Mom, please. We want to see dad, please," The boys beg and plead both their mom and Calvin.

I can't hear anything that was said but I'm reading body language. It's clear that she's trying to figure something out. Suddenly, everyone was looking intently in Stewart's direction.

We all sit there with our mouths open as we witness Stewart picking up Gabrielle for the first time. The sight of Gabrielle and her father together is so emotional even I tear up. Calvin holds Nadine close. It's the last piece of Nadine's puzzle.

Miss Kim

Two weeks later, and it's Manasha's birthday! Of course, I'm having a party for her at my new apartment. We let the kids have the run of the upstairs while the grown folks party downstairs. My parents came early and gave their favorite Grand girl too many presents.

Everyone asks where Mrs. Cheryl is. I lie and tell them she's busy today. Truth is, I didn't invite her because she's still trippin'. It's gotten worse since I've started dating Chris seriously. She keeps asking me if I'm going to let him move in with me like her whole world will tumble and fall if he moves in.

Mrs. Cheryl and I have a toxic, meaning poisonous, venomous relationship now. Every time we are around one another the end result is some kind of argument or fight. I will not have that kind of drama around my baby period, so I'm having fun with the ones truly care about us.

The fun lasts all night with Sakoya and Anthony going at it with their quick wit and raunchy responses. At times, it is a little awkward when Anthony plays with his fresh toothpick looking at me, standing too close to me, and still asking me when he can take me out when Chris isn't around.

Nadine and Calvin are slow dancing in the middle of the room. We are just walking around them.

My brother-in-law is here, but I'm a little worried about him. He has taken Lawrence, his son, out of the hospital early and moved out of the house, leaving my sister home alone with no support. Granted, he moved in the condos right down the street. He can literally see his own front door from his condo window. He's here talking with the guys, soliciting their advice. Don't know if it's all good advice but advice nonetheless.

Even Mrs. B. shows up with a beginner bible for Manasha. We are all having a wonderful time. My old school music is playing, the wine is plentiful, and the food is Chinese. Manasha loves Chinese food. She can even use the chopsticks.

My doorbell rings. I'm thinking its Stephani coming back. When Brandon arrived, she didn't want to ruin the evening so she left. They have been going at it since the birth. Stephani wants Brandon and her son to come home. Brandon still doesn't believe his wife's rape story and why she never told him about it.

When I open the door, Mrs. Cheryl is standing in my hallway dressed to the hilt with her cigarette lit and flask hanging out her purse, drunk out her ass. She walks right in.

"Hey Mrs. Cheryl. How are you? We thought you weren't coming," Standing over my shoulder, Nadine is happy to see her boss.

"You know I wasn't coming! I didn't get invited! I came anyway! Manasha is my friend too! I bought her something."

It is clear to everyone she is loaded, "Where is it?"

"Yeah…where is it? Anyway, I saw all yall's car over here, so I came to see what was going on. I notice you wasn't at work today Dani? What happened? On Friday of all days! No call! No nothing! I should fire your ass!"

My evening is officially ruined. This woman is in my house screaming at the top of her lungs at me with everyone staring in disbelief. Manasha and her nosy friends ran downstairs to see what the ruckus is about.

"Go back upstairs! Mrs. Cheryl come with me outside!"

"Why I got to go outside? Everrybodddy else is in here!"

"It's clear you had too much to drink already…"

"What you scared? Huh Dani? Scared I'm a say something?"

"Say what Mrs. Cheryl? Huh? What you wanna say? Say it loud where everybody can hear you!"

This trick better keep her mouth shut or I will stomp her like grapes in a barrel. Silence.

"Like I said, everybody continue having a good time while my boss and I have a talk in the kitchen."

We get to the kitchen. I swear I want to harm her in such a way, but I can't, this is my daughter's party. What kind of example will I be showing my daughter and all the other kids and adults by behaving like a crazy bitch? The same crazy bitch, that bit a preacher on the neck in church, and was ready to hit this trick in the head with a cast iron skillet.

"Look Cheryl, I don't know what your problem is but you need to get it together. This is my daughter's party, and I truly don't appreciate you coming over here uninvited and then causing a scene! How desperate can you be? Damn!"

"What? You don't have time for me anymore? You through with me…jus like that? You wanna act like what we have isn't real?"

"First of all, keep your voice down! Second we don't have shit! Why you making it out to be more than it is. Get over it already!"

"So you want me to leave while you sit here and entertain your friends. I see Miss Poor-white-beat-up trash is here with what's-his-face, Calvin. Think she's all that now 'cause this one hasn't beat her ass yet. He will too, you just wait Cinda-fuckin'-rella!"

I had to get her out of my apartment. I'm so embarrassed. I can tell Mrs. Cheryl is not trying to leave no time soon. The quicker I get her outside the faster she will leave.

"Nosey-ass Sakoya! Can't understand shit she's talking about. She is as ghetto as they come! Why would anybody want to associate themselves with that braid wearing, fake nail, having Jezebel?"

Bosslady is really pissing me off, however I will remain calm so I can get her to get in her car.

"Since you don't like anybody here, why don't you just leave? Get in the car and go! Nobody wants to hear all that shit you talking okay. Trust me it ain't over. I would never come to your house and try to embarrass you in front of your friends."

"What? C'mon? You gotta be shittin' me. Anthony? Freakin' Anthony? He's one of your *close* friends? He got shit for brains!! I see you two, always laughing, and snickering in the break room. You screwin' him too? Ain't you? Ya'll think I don't know, I know!" She took a drag of her cigarette and blew the smoke out in my face.

"He is still living with his mother!! Oh... I forgot that's how you like 'em. The man you got now still lives with *his* mother! You're so dumb it's unreal!" Mrs. Cheryl took another drink from the small cylinder.

I smacked that drink out of her hand so fast, and just when I about to choke her, Brandon came outside the apartment.

"Dani, you alright? What's going on?"

"Oh Brandon's here. He can come over to party but won't go home and talk to his wife. Who can blame him? I would have moved out too!"

Brandon turns back towards the apartment. I could see everyone listening to us argue outside.

Mrs. Cheryl is speaking loudly so Brandon can hear her. He went back inside.

"How in the world you expect your husband to believe you wasn't cheating on him, but had another man's baby? Oh! Excuse me! Somebody raped her! Where Miss-I-got-it-going-on at? Why isn't she here? Does the boy look like her or me? He don't look like Brandon!"

"Cheryl just leave!" I open her car door.

I can see the light on in the backroom. Calvin, Chris, and Brandon are all in there talking. Mrs. Cheryl zooms in on them too. It's obvious Chris and Calvin, mostly Calvin's, doing all the talking. It looks as if Brandon could kill someone by now because of this hate spewing bitch. She starts again yelling toward the backroom window.

"Brandon, you should have paid more attention to your wife! You was too busy wit yo work! Now she's a-half-crazy-no-baby wanting adulteress!"

Everything stops when Mrs. B. come outside not speaking a word. Mrs. Cheryl immediately stops her tirade, retreats to her car, and peels out of my driveway.

I turn around to find Chris is staring at me from the backroom window.

Chris and I have not really seen or talked each other since my daughter's party. It's almost like he doesn't know what to say, so he's avoiding me saying he's been busy on a job. That could be true, so I don't press the issue. But tonight is our fourth month anniversary, to celebrate we're shooting pool, and eating wings; his idea.

At the back table of the Eight Ball & Wings on Salem, we are having a fun night out. I haven't laughed like this in a long time. We are battling on the table. The score is tied.

I'm just about to break when Chris walks behind me to check my stance. I can feel his package against my backside.

"Would you please quit?! You see I'm trying to bust these balls."

"Yeah, you *are* bustin' my balls!"

"Yeah, I know that's all you want anyway is to get into my Victoria Secrets." The cue smacks hard against the colorful triangle.

"If that's all I want I coulda been had dem secrets! I'm a let you keep your secrets for now," I'm watching as he bends over to take his shot driving in a highball. I wonder if that last statement has anything to do with Manasha's party.

"Whatever! That's why you ain't gettin' none."

I need to distract him from his game. He knocks in another ball. It's his turn again, walking around my way, stepping in close rubbing my body as he walks by.

"Eleven in the corner," lining up his shot; miss.

"That's cool. I'll wait until I have your full attention. Right now, you got a lot going on. I know you have to take care of your sister. Help her find out exactly what happened to her. You said she told the police who she thought the guy might be, right?"

"Yeah, it was the doctor that she was going to see. We still don't know how he got into the house. The police are still questioning him," I walk around the entire table looking for my shot. I gotta beat him.

"Well, that's good, but Brandon is all torn up about it. We talked to him for a while at Manasha's party, but he says he isn't going back home until Stephani gets better."

"Yeah, we are in constant communication, so he knows what's going on with Stephani. He wants to stay away for a while, so she can concentrate on getting back to her old self again. He has a lot he has to deal with himself, feeling guilty like he had some part in all this. Feeling like he shouldn't have waited as long as he did, feeling like he didn't spend enough time with his wife that she sought comfort from another man. Calvin's been going over to his apartment having a few sessions with him."

"I tell you who needs counseling that boss of yours! What was her deal that night?"

I wondered how long it would take him to bring it up. We are having such a great time too.

"I know, I know...Mrs. Cheryl gets a little crazy when she drinks and she felt like I did her wrong by not inviting her."

"So why didn't you invite her?"

This is one of those moments when you find yourself sweatin'. Do I tell this man, this wonderful, caring, fine black man, the truth? "Well, I didn't invite her because I don't want her to get

171

the wrong idea about us. Honestly, she and I have hot, steamy sexual escapades and now she thinks we are in a relationship. She's in love with me."

Or do I just keep my mouth shut and spare this wonderful, caring, fine black man of the trivial pursuits of a lonely desperate woman.

"I know how she gets when she's been drinking, and I just didn't want that around 'Nasha that's all, but it happened anyway."

"But it was like she wasn't just mad about not getting invited."

"Her life isn't all that great right now. That's why she drinks because she is depressed. Her husband, David has been paralyzed from the waist down for the past five years. He drove both of them into a tree on purpose, she was twenty-seven, he was thirty two still in his prime, when it happened."

"Why?"

"Because she was flirting with another man right in front of his face. He blames her for the accident. She still carries tremendous guilt from that. He knows she feels guilty, so he talks to her any kinda way; treats her bad. They live in separate parts of their house. He has young nurses come over and take care of him giving him "special massages.""

"I want one!"

"Shut up pervert! You wanted to know. That's just what happened with her husband. Her childhood was even worse. Her older brother, Everett, used to molest her when she was six. Their parents sent him away, and he blamed her for that."

"Damn! I didn't know it was that deep. Well, then you should be nicer to her."

"Whatever! Let's get back to our date and stop talking about her please."

Miss Kim

I walk behind Chris to check out his stance. As soon as I step behind him, he drops his stick on the table, turns around, and kisses me. Pulling my body on top of his, my stick fell to the floor.

With his eyes open, his kisses are fiery, full with passion, awaking everything in my body; I want him.

"Please get off the table," The waiter looks as if he is annoyed.

Chris lines up his next three shots. One by one the balls fall in just as he calls them.

"Rack'em!"

Chris walks around the table, plants another long sensuous kiss on me, and smacks me on my butt when I bend down to retrieve the balls.

The ride home is full of touching and feeling. My body is overcome with emotion desperately needing his attention. I rub his inner thigh, suck on his earlobe, and kiss his neck. At each stoplight, I beg him to kiss me. I love that biting thing he does.

This is what I'm talking about. Here I am damn near raping this man while he's trying to drive us home! I get too involved. I'm setting myself up to get hurt again. Who knows where this is going? I don't. I really can't take another failed relationship, but I know he likes all this attention I'm giving him. I know that. He seems so sincere. We talk about everything. He listens to me and values my opinion. I know he likes me.

We make it to my apartment. Standing in my living room, we have only the little light shining through my blinds from the light post outside. We lay on the couch, him on the bottom with me on top again. His large hairy chest outlines beautifully through his clothes. His body heat combined with his cologne has me under some kind of spell. I can't stop running my hands over his chest, pressing my body against his. Kissing under his chin; I'm on fire!

He's just looking at me, not saying a word. I'm just about to speak when he flips me over and returns my sexual caresses using his hands to navigate my body's terrain grabbing , and pressing my pelvis against his. As our bodies move in unison to the grinding rhythms we create.

It is hot and heavy on this couch. I can't be a fool about this.

I stop the rhythmic grind and ask, "You got some condoms?"

"No. We won't need them. I'm leaving, just wanted to make sure you got in all right."

Chris stands up, straightens out his clothes, grabs his keys off the coffee table, and heads toward the door. I'm behind him like a lost puppy. I pass a mirror and see my hair is sticking straight up like Don King. I try to comb it down quickly with my freshly manicured nails.

"I thought you were going to stay..."

"No. I have to see my mother, and I do have to work. I'll see you tomorrow. Think about us tonight when you sleep," He pecks my lips and left.

This man has me on a high I've never felt. I'm spinning all around my apartment feeling like turning cartwheels or winning the lottery. He is the one for me. I'm comfortable with him. He is my equal. I had a wonderful time tonight and every night we've seen each other. I like him a lot. It won't be long before I'm in love again.

Another Sunday morning, and I'm up early due to my phone ringing every twenty minutes.

"Hello?"

"You still going?"Stephani is asking.

"Yes, I'm going. Are you?" I'm waiting for a response.

"Well, I'll see you there."

I hang up and make another call.

"Sakoya? You up? Are you coming or not? You know I need you there."

"Yeah, girl I been up. I'm almost ready. I'll come to your house and we can leave together."

Sakoya sounds rested and ready to go. I'm not feeling so ready, but I'm not going to let anything stop me this Sunday. It's time.

"Manasha!! You ready to take your bath?"

Entering the church, I'm so nervous; the last time the saints saw me my behavior wasn't so Christianly.

Members give me big hugs and kisses when I pass them by. My nervousness is slowly fading away as they all welcome me back. I sit with Stephani at our favorite pew. She looks so lonely without Brandon and Lawrence. My heart aches for her. Seeing my sister so broken down again makes me realize why I need to be here today. Not to just pray for myself but for my family also. She perks up when she sees 'Nasha.

"Have you seen Sakoya? She can't ever be on time for nothing."

I'm looking around and see all the regular members smiling back at me, except for the pastor's wife and her mother. They always sit together in the choir stand. They have never liked me, but today is not the day for all that. "Get behind me satan!" My beloved Mrs. B. blew me a kiss from her regular seat. She has been asking me to come back to the church since "the incident". She sends scriptures to me via text every morning.

Rev. Booker and the associate ministers are sitting in their proper seats. Frederick and Chloe were nowhere in sight, "Thank you Jesus!"

The congregation stands to their feet as the deacon reads the Scripture. Manasha is standing on the pew between me and Stephani.

"Nook mommy, Nis Nazeen and Calbin. Mommy!!"

Manasha is pulling my hair trying to get me to notice Nadine and Calvin standing in the doorway. They can't move until after the reading. Once finished, they came to sit with us.

"For a minute, I thought you had chickened out."

I whisper to Nadine trying not to disturb anyone, "Hi Calvin." We wave at him at the end of the pew.

My mother is especially happy to see her daughter and grandbaby back in the church. I can tell by the thousand watt smile she has plastered across her face at this very moment. I want to cry. Everyone is here for me supporting me. I'm all choked up but I promised myself no tears. I'm ugly when I cry, snot everywhere. I don't want that today. This is a joyful occasion. A lost sheep has returned to the safety of the flock "Hallelujah."

Rev. Booker is standing behind the podium, reviewing announcements. None of them pertain to me, so I take this time to check my text messages and my lipstick in my mirror compact. Pastor asks if there were any visitors, no one stands up. He's looking around the sanctuary and spots me. He repeats my thoughts verbatim.

"I am happy to see one of my own has come back to serve the Lord once again, Danielle," I stand up with all eyes on me.

"Sweetheart welcome home. I know you went away with a terrible burden troubling you. I know you went away with both a broken heart and spirit. I know you tried to stay away as long as you could. The devil tried to make you believe the saints would mock you, laugh at you, but you came on anyhow. It doesn't matter how long you stayed gone just as long as you return. Both your parents have raised you and your sister to depend on God. That's why the both of you are here right now. Because you know that amid all your troubles and worries, Jesus will work it out."

I take my seat.

"Baby, we make mistakes. Let no one tell you different."

Another faithful member stands up and welcomes me back. All the church members clap their hands. They are happy to see me, except for the pastor's wife, Mrs. Sarah and her mother Mrs. Martha.

Stephani is scrambling in her purse for tissue; the tears are uncontrollable. I know she's thinking about her present situation. I put my arm around her. She's having a hard time.

Reverend Booker starts his sermon from his words to me. I happen to glance up from the scripture, I lose my breath, and tap Stephani on the shoulder quickly.

Stepping in the church in the smoked gray, tailored to fit suit, his tie, shirt, and shoes complimented his attire, I can't believe my eyes.

It's almost like he's moving in slow motion. All the women, along with the choir director are watching him like a hawk.

"What's up man?" Chris and Calvin shake hands as Chris makes his way between Nadine and me.

"Close your mouth *peanut* something might fly in there."

I'm looking directly at my father who is smiling at me when he sees his hardware buddy come through the church doors.

I made sure my sis was okay then I switch my weight in the seat, so I can talk to my new pew partner. My sister rolls her eyes me.

"I didn't know..." I'm whispering.

"Sssshh!! Please be quiet. I can't hear," Chris put his finger to his mouth shushing me. I turn around in my seat.

My emotions are high, ongoing like a river flowing to no specific destination. They have taken me out my seat. I'm standing, crying thanking the Lord for what he has done for me. One year ago, I was a total wreck letting the devil use me like a puppet.

"Forgive me Lord! Make me a better person!"

Today I'm back with the saints and all my true friends and family are here supporting me no matter what was done in the past. I am loved.

"The doors of the church are open."

Reverend Booker is calling for anyone in need of saving. For anyone who needs assurance that his or her soul will live eternally with Jesus. He is calling.

Shuffling starts in the pew. Nadine heads toward the front of the church. Calvin is right next to her.

The rupture of applause in the sanctuary is thunderous. Everyone is full of joy, witnessing a young couple taking such an important step, accepting the Lord Jesus Christ, together as one is awesome.

Rev. Booker asks if the two have anything to say. Nadine grabs the mic from Calvin. She knows *he* will talk extensively.

"I just wanna say. My grandmother taught me. "You can only know true love when you know Jesus Christ. Two of my co-workers, Dani Thompson and Mrs. B, belong to this church and they always have positive words to say in any situation. I couldn't understand how they just never recognize the bad, so I ask them on separate occasions. How is it nothing seems to bother you? Both had the same response, Faith.

"These angels came to see about me when I was in and out of the hospital. Held my hand and prayed over me, when I was nearly beaten to death. When I decided not to be a victim anymore, they were right there with me attending my first Battered Women's meeting. They both told me everything would be all right, but I didn't believe them at first." Mr. Thompson hands Nadine tissue. She can't hold back her tears, "But they never gave up on me. They say, pray on it girl.

My friend Dani over there always says, 'No matter what, keep getting up'!'" That's what I told her this morning when she was having doubts about coming today." She smiles at me.

"Now today, I am a volunteer at the shelter. I'll finish my classes this quarter and get my associate's degree. I have four lovely children, mine and this man's lovely daughter. We have grown together as a family."

I can see Nadine squeezing Calvin's hand. She's hurting him.

"I just want to say thank you to Mrs. B. and Dani for being positive people in my life. One more thing...I want to be positive like that," She finally hands the mic back to Rev. Booker.

"That's all right. Is there anyone else?" Rev. Booker extends his hand.

He turns to Calvin and asks does he wish to say anything. Nadine gives a subtle glance. He shakes his head "no."

Church adjourns and everyone walks around and shakes Nadine and Calvin's hands. Mrs. B. gives her co-worker the biggest and longest hug. Some of the saints had to walk around Mrs. B. She was just standing in front of the both of them smiling.

Nadine, is surprised to see Anthony walking toward her, they exchange hugs. Anthony gives Calvin a hug also. They talk occasionally at the store.

Stephani receives a note. It was passed to her by an usher. I read over Stephani's shoulder.

"Know that through Christ everything is possible. I challenge you to watch and pray. Watch Him work. Your battle is already won. Give Brandon time to heal, he'll come around. Every child is a blessing from God. No matter how they got here. Remember you asked for a baby. I remember at one time that's all you wanted. Whatever misgivings you have about your baby, will soon vanish away. You keep praying and I'll be praying for you."

Mrs. Sarah

Miss Kim

It's Wednesday. Nothing peculiar happens on hump day; business as usual.

The shop is still buzzing about Nadine and Calvin joining church Sunday morning. The beautiful testimony Nadine gave still sends chills down my spine. Saints from the church have been in and out of the store congratulating her and her boyfriend.

Mrs. B. has been smiling at Nadine all week. Whenever Calvin comes to pick her up for lunch, she gives him a big ol' bear hug.

Nadine says, "Anthony, what were you doing at church? I didn't know you belong there."

With a toothpick in hand, he always had something clever to say, "Aye the unsaved need prayer too! The church is fo' us, the unsaved, ya know! What? I can't go to ya'lls church or something? Just ya'll saved folk can attend?" Anthony is pointing with his toothpick, "Dani invited me."

"Do you know how long ago that was?" I remind him.

"So, what you sayin'? Since you asked me last year, that mean I can't come this year?" He stands directly in front of me, looks me dead in the eye, and starts ranting all over again. I can feel his breath on my face. All I could do was roll my eyes at him because I was glad to see him Sunday.

"Whatever! Anthony we were glad to see you!"

I'm on my way back to the stock room, and it happens, she calls me into her office. Mrs. Cheryl is shuffling papers in her filing cabinet.

"Dani, I'm going to need you to start coming in early Friday and Saturday mornings. I know you can handle the responsibility, right? This is what you want to run the whole show right? Well, the time has come, starting this weekend. We'll be gone away on business. Our plane is leaving after work tomorrow. I'll return Sunday evening. I will call you as soon as I get in. Will this be a problem?" She's asking me nicely with a twinge of sarcasm, "By early I mean about six thirty. The water meter inspector is coming to read the meter. You have to be sure you're here, ok?"

"Sure I'll be here."

"I'm sorry I ruined your party the other night. You know I had too much to drink, and you know how I get when I start drinking. I was already mad because David was in his room getting a massage! I can't do anything about it. I did this to him. I can't control myself...Please forgive me for acting like that. I am truly sorry Dani."

"Whatever," I left her in the office.

I make an appointment with the gynecologist. I really don't like going but it's time, and I need some condoms. The next time Chris and I get hot and heavy, I will be prepared with condoms hidden under each pillow including the couch. The clinic has a huge bowl of free condoms in each room.

"Will seven o'clock, Friday morning be all right?" The voice on the other end of the phone is cheery.

"Yes that will be fine. Thank you."

"Guess what? I just made an appointment to see the gynecologist."

"What for? You ain't pregnant, are you?"

Nadine and my mother are the only ones that ask me that question on a daily basis.

"No girl! That's why I'm going."

"So you can get pregnant?"

Miss Kim

"No. I'm going 'cause it's time for my annual check up, but they give out free condoms and honey I'm gonna stock up."

"Yeah, you need to. The way you talk about you and Christian on the couch!"

Sakoya says she felt like a fifth wheel at my apartment on Thursday night. The truth is Calvin, Chris, Nadine, and myself played a couples games all night, and we uses Sakoya as the referee. We let her play a few rounds of each game, but she isn't good at any of it, so she is better off as the ref. Taboo, the newlywed game, even win lose or draw, she sucks.

We were upstairs away from everyone and she says to me, "I can see you changing." She made sure to reassure me that it was all good. She says, "I can tell you in love with Chris already."

As a matter of fact, she said it was written all over my face. She tells me I only want to go out to the clubs when I'm mad at Chris. Her eyes fill with tears when she says we don't hang out as much as we use to. She admits she has her hands full with her new beau also. Sakoya laughs when she says she thought it would be us hanging out with our boyfriends, going to the beach, and out to eat.

"'But no, it's not us, it's you, Chris, Nadine, and Calvin."

I sense a little jealousy. I can tell she wants to talk longer but I can't. I have to get back to the party. We have been friends forever. Things happen and people change. Sakoya will always be my best friend.

"Look, can we talk about this later? We gotta get back."

"What… Back to your new friends; your new found family?"

"Please Sakoya, I don't have time for your insecurities right now. I'm sorry you feel this way but right now isn't the time."

The atmosphere in the apartment is dismal.

I crank up the music and start pouring the wine. Calvin and Chris step out on the terrace. I follow them to avoid more conversation with my angry best friend.

"Hey babe. What's up Calvin? You have been jittery all-night?"

Calvin takes a deep breath, reaches in his pocket, and pulls out a little black, velvet square box. He presents it to us.

"Man! That's a nice size rock you got there..." Chris says.

"Oh my God!" I can't believe my eyes.

"Half carat, diamond cut. I'm serious about her ya'll," says Calvin.

"I'm speechless; I don't know what to say. But do yo thang, dude. I ain't mad atcha. When you gon pop the question, Christmas?" Chris carefully places the ring back in its casing.

"Man, I've had this for a week now. I'm waiting for just the right moment, ya know like Christmas. Ya know special timing is everything, ya know," Calvin sounds a little nervous.

"Yeah man, I feel you, but you should go 'head on and ask her," stated Chris.

"Maybe I will ask her on Christmas," Calvin hurries and shoves the ring in his pocket. He sees his future wife walking toward the terrace. The two men straighten up, trying to act natural.

"Babe, let's get ready to go. We do have to work tomorrow," Nadine advises her boyfriend.

The men did their manly handshake, as if that wasn't enough, they embrace. Chris and I walk Nadine and Calvin to the door. The two men embrace again.

"Alright then. I'm glad ya'll came to visit. Nadine, don't forget to set your clock please. You can't be late tomorrow. You know I got that appointment. You know crazy lady will have a fit if she knew I switched with you without telling her! Calvin be sure she doesn't stay up too late."

While I'm saying my goodbyes, Chris is telling Sakoya about Calvin's marriage proposal. I came in right at the end of the story.

"Do you think it's the time and place that makes the proposal special? Or is the proposal itself that's special?"Chris is asking a general question.

"Well, I think Calvin should ask Nadine in some lavish extravagant way. She will love that and never forget it plus a great proposal increases his chance of her saying yes."

Sakoya sits there with stars in her eyes. That's her, always wanting the dream, picket fence, house, two and half kids, and a dog.

"Me personally, I think he should go ahead and ask her without any hesitation. Time waits for no one, and we are not promised tomorrow." I spoke up just in case he gets any ideas.

Sakoya calls Jason to come pick her up. Looking a little frustrated because she wants to continue our conversation, but Chris is here and he isn't going anywhere. I make a mental memo to take her out so we can really talk.

The Next Morning

I'm rushing out the door to get to my doctors appointment. Here I am warning Nadine to set her clock, and I'm late myself grabbing my cell phone on the way out the door. I'm not really looking forward to this but we women have to go through this yearly. What I am excited about is the free condoms. Maybe when I show Chris he will be ready to get busy. So far he's been a perfect gentleman, even when he spends the night. Just cuddling, that's all we do.

I call Nadine to make sure she's up. No answer on the home phone, that's a good sign. She is up and on time unlike me. I call the store. No answer there either. It's just six twenty maybe she went to get some coffee from next door. I'll call her a little later.

I arrive at the doctor's office early. I need to get in and out so I can get to work before Mrs. Cheryl calls looking for me. Taking a seat in the empty waiting room, I'm confident they should be calling me right away. I took my phone out to give Nadine one more call before I go back.

"Danielle Thompson," The burly nurse looks around like there are others here. I put the phone on vibrate in my purse, "How long has it been since your last pap?"

Spread eagle on the examining table. I can hear my phone vibrating against something in my purse. I'm lying there thinking that's Nadine calling me to let me know Mrs. Cheryl has already called. Damn! I wanted to be finished with all this so she wouldn't know I wasn't there. Whatever, I'll face her later. She's gonna be pissed and I know it. The phone keeps ringing. It's ringing so much the doctor can hear it too.

"You must be a popular girl."

I just smile thinking, "Shut up and get me off this damn table."

"You can get dressed now."

I'm so glad it's over, and I don't have to come back until next year. I dress quickly and grab two handfuls of condoms. I wait to check my phone until after I schedule my next appointment.

In my car, I dig through all the little square colored cellophane packages to find my phone. I have ten missed calls and several messages. Everyone I know has called, even my parents. I knew something wasn't right, I call Stephani.

"Hey what's up? Why is everybody calling me?"

"Oh Dani! I'm so glad to hear your voice! Mom and dad are here with me. We've been trying to reach you. Where are you?"

"I'm leaving the doctors office. I had an appointment today. Stephani, what's going on?"

"Thank God. Have you talked to your boss Mrs. Cheryl?"

"Nooo she's out of town on business…"

"Who opened the store?"

"Will you just tell me what's going on?"

"Baby, I don't know how to tell you but there's been an accident at the store. It's been on the news all morning. There's been an explosion and the entire store is engulfed in flames. They are still trying to get the fire under control now. Just come over here."

"Oh my God! Oh my God! Oh my God! The store is empty right! They didn't pull anybody out right?"

"Yes, baby they did. They don't know who it is."

"It's Nadine."

Miss Kim

One week later, it's standing room only in the Christ the Solid Rock Baptist Church. People from all over the community heard about the sudden and disturbing death. They came to pay their respects to a beautiful and promising young woman. Nadine Abigail Hughes.

The pale gray sky forms angry clouds. They ache thunderously for a fallen angel. The sun never shows its face on this tragic day. It's unbelievable, inconceivable that heavens gates have open up to welcome one of my closest and dearest friends.

Beautiful flowers surround the urn that holds her ashes. Grieving patrons smile when gazing upon a collage of pictures her grandmother put on display. She holds a scrapbook of her fondest memories of her only granddaughter. We all surmise. She never thought she would bury her best friend.

Placed in the middle of all grandmas collages, Nadine's meek and graciousness is captured in a grand oil painting. It too causes a mixture of happiness and pain. It's Anthony's tribute to his co-worker.

"You's a cool white girl," He repeated many times at the store.

We can see her boys sitting in the middle of the crowded sanctuary with their cousin Billy. He is sitting next to their father Stewart and their new stepmother Rebecca. Stewart's tears were ungovernable. I can only imagine his pain with all the times he treated her so badly; the beatings.

Calvin sat next to Nadine's grandmother. Kaitlin held Gabrielle sitting quietly throughout the services. Mrs. B. couldn't sit down. She prays quietly through her flow of tears pacing the back aisle mourning the newest church member.

Rev. Booker spoke, "I had a chance to talk to Nadine briefly a few weeks ago. In our short meeting, I understood Nadine to be a determined woman. Devoted to her family and friends; She loved them all. Her kids and her grandmother the closest relatives she had, were her life, she described her friends as great. She was proud to be their friend.

Nadine Hughes determined not to let the dark past swallow her soul. If you were here a few weeks ago you would know that Nadine was a battered woman. A beaten woman, but she didn't let that stop her. No, instead she made it her starting point. She became a pillar for all battered woman.

In our conversation, she told me all about her trials but also told me she had forgiven the one that caused her so much pain. In fact, she went on to say had she not lived through those trials she wouldn't be the woman she is today. She was thankful to God for showing her how to care for others, learning selflessness, learning to give of herself without the payback. Thankful for all the love she receives now from other battered women that looked up to her.

Her grandmother told her she could never know true love until she knew God. Miss Nadine made up her mind to seek the Lord. Determined to find true happiness, her soul was saved. Let us rejoice and say Amen! Ain't that comforting to know she didn't leave this life without being saved! If you were here you know she accepted Christ as her Lord and Savior just last week. Right now you can truly rejoice and smile because she *is* with the Lord."

Miss Kim

After the services, we all see Calvin
standing in the middle of the parking lot, watching
the boys, Stewart, Rebecca, and Gabrielle pull off in
their minivan. That too is hard to watch, him
standing there watching his family just vanish. One
minute he is planning his proposal, the next his
fiancé to be is dead. Watching Calvin standing
there crying with that black box in his hands. I
wonder if he asked himself, "Why didn't I ask her?"

It was early December, when the store exploded and burned to a crisp. I need a plan quick because I'm jobless with no prospects. Nadine's death has caused me to reevaluate my life. I'm scared.

My relationship with Chris is flourishing, spending as much time as we can together. He's working long hours and taking care of his mother who is back home. Our time is limited.

I'm cool with that. We really have been enjoying each others company with out the pressure of sex. We have much in common, a lot of the same things like board games, backgammon, checkers, scrabble, etc. You name it, we play it. We often play the kiddy games too so 'Nasha can play with us. She adores Chris. I like this slow getting to know pace.

Don't get me wrong. We have been close to consummating our relationship but the timing is never right. That's a sign for me to focus my energy on something else like a career.

Death really puts things in perspective. I can no longer wait to start my own shop. The time is now, but I have to crawl before I walk, so I call my brother-in-law and became his nanny.

Brandon is still living in the high-rise condos down the street from his home he shares with Stephani. He isn't sure he's ready to go home and face everything, especially his wife. He doesn't know how he feels. It's been three months, since he found out Lawrence wasn't his son; he didn't care. Brandon took his son from the hospital and hasn't been home since.

Manasha and I spend most of our time over at Brandon's condo taking care of Lawrence. We have specific instructions not to take the baby to see Stephani. If I do, he will not invest my venture. I just pray over that situation and let the Lord handle it.

He loves, adores, and desperately misses his wife, but she's ask him to believe a story that sounds so far-fetched. Wants him to ignore the fact she has had another man's baby and kept it secret from him for at least nine months, should he forgive her or not? This is all we talk about all day long. I know he's hurting, so all I do is listen. I let him draw his own conclusion on his own terms. He's back to being a work-a-holic.

FloTu Industries is launching a new product. It requires Brandon to spend long hours at the office. Until now, he has managed fatherhood and work habits splendidly. He even has a small nursery in his office equipped with all the essentials for Lawrence. However, he needs more help. That's where we come in.

Manasha helps me watch her baby cousin. She's already got that motherly instinct. While she's entertaining Lawrence, I'm running my ideas about my shop by Brandon. He is the tool I need to make my dream a reality. If anyone can help me, it's him. He is the vice president of one of the largest companies in the surrounding area.

One night after putting both Manasha and Lawrence in bed, Brandon and I sat down and talked in-depth about what I want to do. He listened to every minor detail of my outline. I prepared it myself thoroughly remembering the important facts from seminars I attended in the past. I had charts, graphs and figures explaining in full design what my goals were and how I intend to achieve them. My intensity is deep, my hunger is ravenous, and Brandon can tell as he is taken by surprise. It's written on his face. Every idea I have includes a folder with facts, numbers, contacts, etc. He knows I'm ready. In the middle of my presentation, my phone rings. I ignore it because this is more important.

I answer all his questions. Show him all the projections. I determined the most vital in this venture. I am in businesswoman zone, and I know Brandon likes what he hears. After the presentation, "Well, what do you think bro-in-law?"

"Let's make some calls," I'm jumping for joy and dancing around his lavish apartment checking my messages. Brandon grabs two beers from the frig.

"Hey, where are you going? It's almost one."

"I'm here all-day brah. It's your turn to watch them. I'll be back in a couple of hours."

While I let my car warm up, I call the number left on my phone. I know who left this message, and I really shouldn't call back, but I need closure.

"Aye Can I see you?" A familiar voice asked.

"Don't do this."

"I know...baby, but I can't stop thinking about you. You shouldn't make me crave you like this. I have to wait too long to see you, if you would just quit playin' and c'mon in, we wouldn't have to go through all this. The last time I called, you didn't call back. You must have been with your man, that's cool, that's cool."

"Look, I told you when we started this, we just have *our* fun. That's it. No quality time. No strings. No drama. You said you could handle that.

Miss Kim

Things have changed, I gotta man now. I cannot keep seeing you. You know all this, so why are you acting like you don't understand. No more late night creepin'! This *is* it!"I was serious.

"You can rest yo' neck while you on the phone talkin' all crazy! Just bring your fine ass over here!"The phone went dead.

I don't know why I'm so turned on right now. I shouldn't feel this way, but I do. I can't help it. The aggressive manner, the forbidden force between us consuming me completely like a wild cat devouring his prey. Thinking to myself stirs something deep in my vaginal cavity. My phone rings again.

"Aye, I know you in love with ol' boy, so after this, I won't bother you again. You still comin'?"The familiar voice was back on the line.

" Yes, I can't stay long and this *is* the last time."

"I know how long you been saying that...almost two years now. Just hurry up."

Miss Kim

Stephani is standing in her front door watching us get out of the car.

"Hi aunt Stevie! How are you feeling?" Manasha is learning more phrases.

Stephani hugs her tightly, "I'm feeling great 'Nasha. You want a cookie?"

"Oh yes, I do. Thank you, thank you."

I walk through the door with Lawrence all bundled up. Stephani grabs him quickly cradling him close. I put both diaper bags on the counter.

"Hey big sis! I brought you somebody."

"Dani thank you for bringing him over. Does Brandon know you're over here?"

"Yes, I told him we were coming over. Stephani he doesn't hate you. He just wants you to get better."

The police kept him informed of what's been happening in your case. Since Mr. Scott's arrest, they told him exactly what happened to you. He confessed to everything. He is also wanted in Chicago, so you can relax now that the truth is out in the open."

"Does he know I didn't have an affair? He probably thinks I deliberately got pregnant. I didn't do anything like that," Stephani is whining like she did when we were small.

"Stephani relax. The police told Brandon the doctor drugged you. I filled in the blanks from what you told me and everything made sense."

She is relieved and pleasantly surprised by the biggest smile she's ever seen is finally staring back at her. The foulest odor permeated the entire room. I found Stephani's over excitement for changing her son's first nasty diaper disturbing.

We spent most of our time talking in detail

about my plans, and how I laid it all out to her husband. She asks questions I hadn't thought about and neither did Brandon. I wrote them down. Stephani and I talk business all the time. She always gives sound advice. I let her know Brandon is on board and she agrees. We decide not to waste any time. We will start the plans in motion first thing Monday morning.

My sister wants to know what is happening with my new beau, Christian.

"He is so sweet. We have spent almost everyday together since the play. I didn't get a chance to tell you it was him who sent the ticket and backstage pass. He was there at the hospital visiting his mother when you were having the baby. She's home now. He's excited about that. Her cancer is in remission."

Before I knew it I am rambling on and on about Chris. My sister is grinning at me like she just swallowed a canary, but I don't care.

"He is finishing a building he's been working on for awhile. He said he might wait a while before starting the next contract. You know he can do that because he a boss too! He says he wants to spend more time with me and 'Nasha. Holla atcha girl!" I'm strutting around the room like I just won the lottery.

Stephani's eyes are wide, still grinning, "Girl you is in love! Sickening love! Uuuuugh! You got the cooties!" She sounds like the pestering brat she has always been.

My sister is back. Out of the depression, the dark cloud has been lifted from her sky blocking her sun.

I hug my big sister tighter and longer before we left her house. Lawrence and his mom were still standing in the doorway as I look through the rearview mirror.

It is time for them to know one another.

I call Chris to see if he wants to watch an old school scary movie trilogy. The Birds will promptly start at eight o'clock followed by Psycho and Jaws. "Don't be late!"

I then left messages on all Brandon's voice mails.

"Hey, I have an emergency. I'm all right, but you have to pick Lawrence up from Stephani's," I was trying to sound sincere through my slyish grin.

"Call me if you need me."

Manasha is coloring yet another masterpiece for the wall. The phone in the apartment rings.

"Hey, girl. Are you busy? Do you have company?" Sakoya needs undivided attention at all times.

"What's wrong with you?"

"Every time I try to talk to you, someone is always around. Seems we never talk...like we used to. First, Mrs. Cheryl...where is she anyway?" Sakoya interrupts her own speech.

"I don't know. The police never found her or her husband. When they went to their home it was vacant. Everything is gone.

"Does the police think she had something to do with the explosion?"

"Yeah, since no one has heard anything from them. The police came to Brandon's apartment building to question me. They want to know the last time I saw her...."

Just thinking about that whole ordeal again makes me nauseous and nervous. I can feel a large lump forming in my throat.

"I told them that she asked me to come in early on Friday and Saturday. She said she was going on a business trip, and she was leaving Thursday night."

"She asked you to come in early? You never told me that. Girl, that bitch was trying to kill you! Dani...Dani...Are you there?"

Paralyzed on the side of the bed, I can't believe I'm hearing from someone else what I've known all along. I didn't want to face the fact that she actually was trying to kill me. I can't speak. Nadine's beautiful face is so vivid in my recollections. It should have been me instead of my good friend.

"Mommeee...Don't cry. Mommmeee peeeze," Manasha is hugging my leg.

I put the phone back to my ear, "I'm sorry. Anyway, let's talk about something else. What's up with you?"

"Oh, that's Chris. He just pulled up. I'm sorry, Sakoya I'll call you as soon as the movie is over. Please forgive me. I know you wanna talk, and we will I promise."

Manasha beat me to the door. She is ready for him to come in and sweep her off her feet like prince charming in the Disney movies. My daughter thinks he is the best thing since peanut butter and jelly.

"Hello, Chris."

Manasha pushes me out of the doorway, so he can see her first. In true Chris fashion, he picks Nasha up and swings her around and gives her the biggest hug. Once she lands on the ground, he hugs and kisses me.

"Where's my puppy?" This is true Manasha fashion, accented with her hands on her hips.

"Oh I'm sorry. I told Santa to get him for you because you've been good all year. Is that ok?"

"Ok," Manasha goes back to coloring.

"Did you talk to Brandon about your plans?"

"Yeah, he made a few calls last week. My proposal got the green light, but we have to find another location. He said someone else had already bid on the lot Mrs. Cheryl's store was on. That sucks! I really wanted that lot."

Chris and I talk about everything; my sister and her recovery, and my new job venture with my brother-in-law. He offers his help in finding a new, inexpensive lot.

We are both pumped on all the good news. He tells me his mother will have a full recovery and her hair is growing back. We talk all night about the possibilities of my dreams becoming reality. Chris' dreams of having his mother around to see his children whenever he has some will come to pass. The doors that will open up for us in the future, it's almost like we are planning our lives together on this night. This is the night we can say is the beginning of our true commitment to each other. I am so in love with him and our relationship.

The supreme, deluxe, extra cheese pizza with twenty hot wings, two ranch dressings washed down with seven up, hits the spot, but the movie is not scary at all.

All conversation has ceased. Chris is sitting between my legs as I massage his temples and scalp.

"I want you and 'Nasha to come spend Christmas with us."

"We would love to! If you spend New Years with us, deal?"

"Deal."

Today was truly a great day. My stars are aligning; the ducks in cadence are forming in a row. Excitement is keeping me up with so many positive thoughts running through my mind all at once. I haven't felt this way in awhile, and it feels good.

The rollercoaster ride of pure bliss I rode the last month is clearly over. On 23 December, I open a letter that reads:

> *Danielle,*
>
> *I love you. Please don't hate me. I tried to tell you, didn't know how to tell you but the timing was never right. When I had the chance, the words just wouldn't come out. I guess I was afraid of what you might say. I sent you this letter because I couldn't tell you face-to-face.*
>
> *I know you are mad right?...*
> *Okay...Ok...Here goes.*
>
> *Quinton has a new truck route, in Chicago. He asked me to move with him. I thought about it, thought about it, thought about it and decided to go.*
>
> *Dani, I don't have kids, work in the medical profession. I can get a job at any hospital. I won't be that faraway, we can visit every weekend if we wanted to. That's what we were doing anyway. Since you hooked up with Chris, we hardly ever see each other. I'm not jealous or nothing. I just want a life too.*
>
> *Please understand. I will call you with all the details. Tell everyone bye and hi for me. Kiss 'Nasha and tell her I'll see her soon.*
>
> > *Love*
> *and my Best Friend,*
> > > *'Koya*

I keep Koya's letter in my purse. Every now and then I read it silently to myself reminding me how busy I was. So busy she had to write me a letter. In such a short period of time I have managed to lose two of my closet friends. No, Sakoya isn't dead, but she isn't close anymore. We can't just go to breakfast like we used to or sit up and talk for hours while drinking cheap wine. Good times, good times.

Christmas at the Mitchell's is boring. Maybe I'm just a bit biased toward their way of celebrating. At our house, we play family games all night long, having a ball. Here at the Mitchell's it's a little more subdued; too quiet.

Chris' mother, Belinda Mitchell, 48 is a kindhearted woman thrilled about being home for the holidays sitting comfortably in her easy chair, reading the latest issue of O. The medical supplies and equipment dominate the space around her.

Watching his mother struggle to do the smallest task is saddening. Still in much pain, Belinda keeps her happy spirits up. Relaxing in her new pair of pajamas, she worries about her hair. A sassy little woman tells me of the days when her hair was long and thick. With all the meds she has to take, she wonders if it will grow back as strong.

Chris spent most of his time tending to his mother getting her meds ready for the next round while I sit in the den watching football with his brothers, James, 26 and Kyle, 18 and "uncle Blu," 52.

Manasha is playing with her new friends, Myles and Jessica. They are James' children. They immediately take Manasha to the Christmas tree where all the new toys are. My daughter is telling her new found buddies that she's getting a puppy for Christmas.

There is a small spark of excitement when my sister calls with the news of her and Brandon trying to work things out. It isn't a surprise. That was part of my plan when I came up with the idea of working for Brandon. Along with implementing my work ideas with brother-in-law, I would lure the two back together. Hence, visiting Stephani with Lawrence, then the emergency, I knew that night would change everything. All they had to do was open up and talk. Now, everything will change, again for the better. I'm hoping the worst is over.

Afraid not, I'm out of a job, rent is past due, and I'm stuck here in this den on Christmas day watching football.

Miss Kim

It's New Years Eve.

Chris keeps his promise to spend it Manasha and I. Eager about night watch service, he invites his entire family to attend as well. He has never brought in the New Year in church before. I'm not sure he went to church at all when younger. He told his family about the services at Christmas dinner. They all agreed to join us.

"Do you know how Night Watch services started?"

"No Chris I don't. How did Night Watch start?"

"On December 31, 1862 known then as Freedom's Eve, the black communities gathered in churches and private homes all across the nation awaiting the news of the Emancipation Proclamation to hear it had become law. At the stroke of midnight, January 1, 1863 all the slaves of the Confederate states were declared legally free."Chris was proud of his black history moment.

"Wow, I never knew that. I've been going because our parents made us." I laughed.

Manasha runs to her Papa as she enters the church. It is about ten forty five. Chris didn't expect to see so many young people at the service. His mother, brothers, and uncle were already sitting together.

Of course I sit next to my sister who is alone on our favorite pew. Lawrence's belongings are under the pew but the baby isn't in sight. I check Mrs. Claudine's regular seat. There he is. I see Manasha running to her grandmother trying to hold the baby and sit on my mother's lap too. I need to get her before she hurts someone.

I spot Anthony sitting in the back of the

church. I can't believe he is here. When I ask him to come, he acted like he had so many parties to go to. Seeing him is a pleasant surprise; we smile and wave. I check Mrs. B's seat to make sure she is here; she is. I don't know why I thought any different. She's always here.

The choir sings beautifully. They always rehearse new songs for this particular evening. The spirit is uplifting. Everyone is grateful for seeing one year go and ready to greet the New Year with hope and faith just like back in the day.

In the midst of all the singing and praising, Rev. Booker passes the mic around for any and all saints who want to testify about the goodness of the Lord. He wants to know and share with everyone how the Lord blessed this year. He wants to know if there are saints wanting to do something for God. He passes the mic to anyone not ashamed to tell the good news.

Saints jump up like popcorn. There are testimonies so intense, eye opening, and heartfelt. I feel the blessings as each one testified. The Lord is doing so many great wonders in everyone's life. People even thank Him for the suffering they endured this year, because without it, they would have never grown closer to God.

I cry so hard when thinking of my year, my job, and Nadine and Sakoya all gone. Not to mention my boss tried to kill me. She's more than just my boss, but I'm determined not to let anything stop me. Everything happens for a reason, so I dry my tears and hold my head up high thanking the Lord for everything. I can't stop smiling and listening to the praises. I know I have been out of church too long. I want to speak but have a little apprehension.

Miss Kim

Calvin walks through the doors of the church. My heart nearly jumps out of my chest. I know that's my sign from Nadine to get up and speak for the Lord. I stand up and wait for the mic. Chris stands with me.

"Happy New Year saints. First, I want to apologize to Rev. Booker and to you saints for the unchristian behavior I displayed last year. There is no excuse for that. I prayed about it, and the Lord has forgiven me. I hope you can find it in your hearts to forgive me also."

Amen's were heard all over the sanctuary. I try to give the mic back to the usher, but Chris has something to say. Rev. Booker didn't rush Chris but reminds him to keep it brief. The time is drawing near to midnight. Chris will be the last person to speak.

Brandon walks in just as Chris is beginning. After kindly removing his son from my mother's grasp, he takes his seat next to his wife and puts his arm around her.

"Uumm...Happy New Year saints. I am not a member, but I have been visiting here for a couple of months now. I want to thank the Lord for letting my mother come home from the hospital. She's sitting with my brothers and uncle in the back."

The saints turn their attention to the woman with the scarf tied fashionably around her head.

"When my mother was diagnosed with cancer this summer, I was more scared than she was. She always remained faithful and strong through the surgeries and chemotherapy; I marvel at her strength. I want to say thank you Jesus for saving my mother. The cancer is in remission."

The saints clap and praise the Lord. Chris can hardly speak, clearing his throat with small beads of sweat forming on his forehead.

"I know God sends his angels when you are in need or in trouble. He placed this lady in my life right when I thought there was no hope for my mother," He then turns his attention to me, "She always speaks of the Lord and his grace. Without her by my side, I don't know what I would've done. I just want to take this time to let everyone know Dani is an angel, my angel God sent just for me."

When all the Amen's ceased Chris faces me, looks deep into my eyes then knelt down on one knee,"Dani, please will you marry me?" Chris places a diamond ring on my finger.

The sanctuary is quiet, and I have to pee. The tears start flowing when I see it; the ring. It's the same ring Calvin wanted to give Nadine. I glance over at Calvin. He winks at me.

"Yes!"

The church members clap and cheer. The organist plays happy music for us.

There is only ten minutes left in 2007. Rev. Booker requests for everyone to find a spot on the floor. All eyes are closed and every knee is bowed.

Night watch service is over, and I'm engaged, Hallejuhah! All the saints congregate and fellowship with each another. Many came to us with words of encouragement, hugs, and kisses. They are truly happy for us.

Mrs. B. is all smiles again wanting to see the ring. Her mouth falls open when I extend my left hand. She gives Calvin a big hug too. She hasn't seen him since Nadine's funeral.

"Keep your head up. The Lord has great works in-store for you," says Mrs. B.

Mrs. B. sits down with Stephani for a moment waiting for her turn to ogle and hold the baby. Her heart is in the right place, but we all know she is trying to see who the baby looks like.

The church has cleared out. I see Anthony leaving out the back door. I want to thank him for coming, but everyone is waiting on me.

Manasha is asleep in her papa's arms. My parents are happy with the events that have occurred. We all walk to the back of the church to have both our family's meet.

"Dani, baby you looked so surprised. Didn't you know he was going to ask you?"

My mother in her ankle length fur walks with her arm around my waist. I lost all train of thought when I saw Anthony's car. Our eye's met for what seemed like some hypnotic trance.

"Dani?"

"No. I had no clue mom. My head is still spinning. I keep pinching myself to make sure I'm not dreaming. I can't believe it! You know this is Nadine's ring?" I show my mother the ring again. For the first time, I can see my mother is proud.

"Yes, I know. Isn't it gorgeous? I couldn't believe it when I saw it the first time either. I believe she wants you to have it."

"The first time…what are you talkin' bout mama?"

"Well, you know Chris shops at your dad's hardware store just about every day. I think he gets all his supplies from there now. Anyway, he and your father have gotten to know each other pretty well. In fact, he asked your father if could he marry you then, of course, I had to meet him. He is a good man with a good head on his shoulders. We gave him our blessing."

The next day my sister and I talk on the phone for hours. We can't control ourselves. We are giddy like when we were kids going to Kings Island with our parents for the first time. With so much excitement happening around us, we are both bubbling with joy. Stephani's joy sounds more erotic than mine. She begins her sappy gossip with her and Brandon spending their first night together since the whole baby ordeal.

"Everything was a little awkward at first. There's a lot of nervous tension until Brandon sees the new bed in our bedroom. I can tell he feels more at ease, looking around the room seeing that nothing has changed, so I go into our bathroom and change into something more comfortable. There weren't many words said between us after I came out in my oily birthday suit and black patent leather stilettos. I poured his favorite cabernet sauvignon that I was saving for this special occasion. I turned the heat up to knock the chill out of the air, learned that from Dr. Ruth, so we will be comfortable in our raw, unadulterated nakedness.

I sashay back into the bedroom still in the buff with the wineglasses. He can't keep his eyes off me. I make sure to bend over a couple times for no apparent reason. I undressed him slowly. We didn't speak. We just looked into each others eyes the entire time almost like we didn't need any words.

Dani when I take off his shirt, his scent was like an aphrodisiac to me. I realized how much I miss my husband and how much I am still in love with him. Girl I was ready!

Brandon can't wait any longer either, taking his pants off quickly, and laying me on the bed. He's kissing me so passionately. We've NEVER kiss like that before! We were both so hot for each other I can't even explain it. Our bodies moved together in a sensual rhythmic motion. Our skin fused together creating a passion we had never experienced before. Oh my God! Dani it was so wonderful! Honey, that's just the foreplay!"

"Sister, are you sure you want to tell me all this?"

"Shut up and listen! I whisper "I love you" in his ear and open my legs inviting him in to rekindle, revisit, and reacquaint himself with me, his loving wife. Sis, that thang was anaconda-like!"

Don't know if I want to hear anymore, but I know she is so excited about her husband's return that I have to indulge her. She's never been this excited about sex, ever, plus I aint gettin' none right now so I will live vicariously through her. I encourage her to let it out. My sister hasn't been this happy since I don't know when.

"You know that's how we like'em!"

"Dani, you would have been so proud of me girl. My uninhibited sexual prowess overcame me and I took charge! I rolled him on his back and became that sex kitten he always wanted. He let me have my way.

After planting kisses all over his neck, throat, under his chin and to his lips I move downward and that's when it happened. Honey, that anaconda came alive again and hit me in the forehead!"

Remembering all the dirty books he likes, the movies he watches in his office, and all the times he woke me in the middle of the night to try something different, I became his fantasy freak, twirling, stroking doing everything I can to his strong hard pole. I surprised myself, giving in to the passion, and letting all the frigidness go."

"Is frigid-ness a word?"

Miss Kim

"Yes it is. Are you listening to me? I let that part of me go. It's so liberating. That's why I had to tell you. You have called me frigid, cold, stand-offish all of my life. Now I can say you were right, but now I'm a superfreak just like you!"

"Is standoff-ish a word?"

"You need to read more."

Since Chris' proposal, I have been busy planning my fairytale wedding.

"I know you want everything, but you'll have what we can afford."

My mother always chimes in when I get too carried away with the plans. She and my sister both vetoed the chocolate fountain at the reception. They say it's an accident waiting to happen to me because I'm the clumsy one.

Although I share all my plans and ideas with them, I still wish I had my two closest friends to help me. They both have their own style. Both of them would have so many great ideas. Nadine will not be in my bridal party. I don't know if Sakoya wants to be in my wedding or not. I wasn't there for her when she needed me, so why would she? She hasn't gotten her measurements, shoes or anything. It's now April only two months until the big day. We talked for at least two hours, when I called to tell her every detail about the proposal at the church, the ring, and everything.

"It's Nadine's ring. After her sudden death, Calvin couldn't bring himself to take it back. He held on to it. When Chris told him he was going to ask me to marry him, he insisted Chris take Nadine's ring. Calvin felt like she would approve. That would be their wedding gift to us from them."

"Oohh, I wish I could have been there to see it."

"Yeah, you coulda, but nooo you want to be movin' away, shackin' up, and playin' house!"

This is my way of letting her know that she hurt me by moving away so abruptly. I understand her decision, but I don't agree with it. However, I do want her to have the same kind of love that I have. Sakoya tries to ease my mind by telling me all about her new adventures. She already has a job for a private doctor, a Podiatrist.

"Well, that's wonderful. What else have you been doing?"

Sakoya goes on to tell me she has gone on a road trip with Quinton. Our conversation turns into a sentimental love fest. We went back and forth with wonderful stories of our men. This is the first time we have been in love at the same time.

"The wedding day is set for June 21st. You need to get your measurements taken! You know I hate your last minute crap! When are you coming back?"

"Calm down, I see you have your pre wedding jitters. I keep telling you we are not that far from each other. I can come home whenever you need me. Why did you pick June?"

"Chris has two projects he's working on. They won't be complete until then. After those projects are finished, he will take time off until we come back from our honeymoon. That gives me, mom, and Stephani enough time to plan my grand wedding event of the year."

I am rubbing it in, so she will want to come home sooner and be apart of everything.

"Has Chris moved in with you and 'Nasha yet?"

I can tell by Sakoya's tone she is trying to ignore my taunting. She starts smacking on candy in my ear. She knows smacking gets under my skin like fingernails on a chalkboard.

"No. He has some of his clothes here, but he still keeps an eye on his mother. We will wait until we marry. We have gone this long without living together, so why rush it? We still haven't done it yet," I know this bit of juicy info will shock her.

"You lyin'! What? What's up with that? Girl, is he gay?" Sakoya starts laughing at her little quip.

"Is yo momma gay! You know we have been intimate, hot sizzlin' intimate, but we just haven't yet. His work, basically taking care of his mother and uncle, and nearly raising his brother's kids, we don't have a lot of time alone. Changing the subject, remember I told you I can't get the old store. So, I put a bid in for a place downtown, and I think they are going to accept my offer. I won't know until some time in May. I have been to a couple of banks to see if I can get a loan. None of the banks will give me one, so I have been extremely busy to even think about sex."

"Yeah well, it doesn't sound right to me. I know you got a little stand by somewhere. I don't know what Chris is doing. Maybe *he* is for real, but you...Who is he?"

"Who is who?"

"You know your little stand by. Your cutty buddy who is it?"Sakoya is cutting her eyes at me like she knows something I don't.

"Sakoya shut up! You don't know what you are talking about. Ain't it time for you to get off the phone now? Just call me when you are in town."

I chuckle at Sakoya's little remark. She's so funny. If she only knew my so called cutty buddy is my boss and she tried to kill me. I'm not chuckling anymore.

"*What* time you coming home?"

Chris yells up the stairs at me as if he is in a football stadium calling plays.

"It shouldn't take that long. Are you sure you don't want to go?"

Giving myself the once over in the mirror before leaving the bedroom. I must admit I'm looking rather scrumptious in my Nicole Miller strapless twist bodice royal blue dress with Michael Kors strap pumps and purse.

"Who's going to watch the kids? You go ahead and have a good time. We'll be all right. They got everything they need pizza and chips."

Chris positions himself on the couch with his beer, TV remote, and phone. Manasha, Myles, and Jessica are all camped out in Manasha's room. They have, Brownie, Manasha's new puppy upstairs too. They laugh so loud when she barks.

"I'll call and check in bye baby and listen for them kids."

I kiss everybody before leaving. Truthfully, I'm a little apprehensive about going to this opening. Staring at the first art opening invitation, it states the festivities will start promptly at nine; it's eight fifty now. I'm in the car, nervous, on my way to show support to my artistic friend. Arriving at the art museum, the parking lot is packed. Now, I'm really nervous. I'm here to show support to my friend and that's all. It's been a while since I've seen him. As a matter of fact, I haven't seen him since Nadine's funeral. Just a quick visit and I'm out.

The elegant museum is full with people wandering about. Whispering, pointing, and gazing at the fine art displays on the walls, handmade pottery, sketches, photos and paintings. It's all so picturesque just the way he envisioned it. Looking around I'm amazed, stuck in the awe-ness of someone's dream. He made it come true.

Soft music plays throughout the white halls with only art as its color. It's breathtakingly beautiful. The champagne fountain flows freely into my plastic flute as I peruse the canvases slowly checking the signatures of each. They are signed the same. Each piece is mesmerizing. I know he's good, but this is phenomenal.

"You like what you see?"

All of a sudden a pair of strong arms wraps themselves around my waist. His body is pressing tightly against mine. He nuzzles his face against the back of my neck. I can smell his Giorgio Armani. The familiar sent buckles my knees for a moment until I break away from his intoxicating embrace.

"Anthony, please don't do that."

The first thing I notice is his gold tooth is gone, and he has straight, white teeth. His hair is cut short wearing a navy pinstriped double breasted suit looking like he just stepped out of Ebony Man magazine. It's Anthony modified.

"Why? Is your man here?" He let go abruptly.

"No, he is not here," I'm looking around making sure no one saw him hugging on me.

"But...Anyway, Anthony this is wonderful! Is this all your work?"

"Every piece, yeah, since the store burned, I had to do something. You know tryna come up a little bit."

Anthony moves closer to me really invading my personal space, but I don't move. He sweeps a stray hair away from my face.

"I remember what you said about wasting my talent. How the Lord would take it away if I didn't use it, so you could say you helped me with my vision."

He strokes my face with the back of his hand.

"Stop that!"

"C'mon"

Anthony takes my hand leading me to a painting that I can't believe is hanging before me. I've never seen anything like it. While I'm marveling at this rarity, Anthony puts his arm around me again, but I didn't pull away this time.

The painting is a sky view of the Reed's Greeting card store, every detail, painted flawlessly. I want this picture hanging in my new establishment one day.

"I want this one."

"Isn't it beautiful?!" Another familiar voice rings into the air jolting my body away quickly from Anthony's subtle embrace.

"Hi Mrs. B! I didn't know you were here too! It's good to see you. Praise the Lord," I hug the elderly saint.

"Yes, you know I support my people. Look at that. The sight of the old store gives me a chill. You know I work at the library now."

While I'm conversing with Mrs. B., Anthony sneaks away to talk with other on-lookers.

"Congratulations! I'm still working on trying to get the building downtown for my store. I couldn't get the old store."

"That's all right. When one door closes, another opens. Just call me when you get settled. It's nothing to talk about at the library. Tell Anthony I will look for him to be at church

Sunday."

The well-dressed Mrs. B. made her way out the door. She collects her fur coat and several purchases on the way out.

Anthony looks so professional standing there talking to potential buyers, almost unrecognizable. I walk to the rear of the gallery where the paintings were even more uplifting and powerful. There's a typed memo for each piece, describing it, and what inspired him to paint it.

Reading some of the carefully written literature, again it astounds me. The way he acted at work is nothing at all compared to the man, the artist, the entrepreneur I see tonight. He is on his way to something marvelous. "Damn he fine!"

Anthony must have seen me head for the door when he stops me by blocking my path.

"Come with me. I want to show you something."

"No. I have to leave. Chris and 'Nasha are waiting for me."

"Oh, so ya'lls one big happy family now...huh? One big, happy unit!"

His clever sarcasm lets me know he's still jealous of Chris. It also let's me know why I want to slap him most of the time.

"It's not late. Call him and tell him you'll be home after the presentation. Look, if you call now he won't be mad. It's not even ten o'clock yet."

This is the moment I always make the wrong decision. I know I should go home, but I'm really having a great time. It's early, and I don't do this often. This is my friend, my co-worker. Why am I tripping like that anyway?

"Aye, you gotta be proud of me! You just

gon' leave yo' friend like that? This is my night. You thought all I was going to do is stay in my mother's basement smoking, right? Well, just stay a few more minutes, so I can prove some more stuff to you."

I make the call. Anthony is leading me through the gallery to the backstairs.

"Where are we going? What about you're showing? The buyers?"

Now, I'm worried because we in the back of the showroom. No one can see us, and no one knows we're back here.

"Close your eyes."

"I don't have time for this!"

"Damn! Don't close'em then!"

Anthony opens the door. We step into a spacious office, very classy. He extends his arms presenting his private haven. Each wall, hand painted by him, including the ceiling.

The decor was something out of a magazine. Again my mind races as I see my portrait, my face displayed in his office. It is the same portrait he painted for me two years ago. The same one that is hanging in my apartment. This is overwhelming. "Oh my God. This is unbelievable."

"Anthony I do have to leave...It's getting late."I'm so nervous right now.

"You'll be at home with time to spare. Relax, he got you like that?" Anthony walks around me closely. His scent drives me crazy inside.

"So that's the type you like huh? I didn't have enough money for you then, but I got it now. Do I have a shot at taking yo fine ass out now?" He kissed the nape of my neck.

"We don't have time to go through this. Chris and I just happened. I don't even know when we started dating."

"Don't lie. You know exactly when you started. I know...That's when you stopped coming to see me...Well, that's not true. You *still* come to see me."

"Do you remember the first time you *came* to see me? No pun intended."

"Anthony, please do we have to do this? Tonight of all nights? C'mon."

He pulls me close, "Kiss me."

"Let me go. I'm marrying Chris. Anthony, I'm not in love with you."

"Kiss me."

"You have a hard time listening. I'm leaving."

I leave Anthony standing in the middle of his haven alone.

That was a close call. It took all I had not to kiss him. Why do I want to? I have a wonderful man at home waiting on me. After starting the car, I reminisce recalling all the offbeat things Anthony would do and say to get my attention. He's the first person I met when I went on my interview with Mrs. Cheryl.

He was such a jerk. I remember the night we had the conversation about his talent. How I said he was wasting it. I didn't think he was paying any attention to me back then when it came to his talent, but he paid much attention to me. My memories unfold on the way home.

One day, Anthony left his check at the store. Mrs. Cheryl asked me to take it to him on my way home. It was raining.

When I got there Anthony came to my car with the umbrella up, so I wouldn't get wet. I was just going to drop the check off but he invited me in. I was reluctant, but I went in anyway directly to his mother's basement.

I don't know how he gets me to do things. It's like he has some kind of spell on me. Just like in the museum he wanted me to stay with him. Knowing full well I shouldn't. I called my fiancé, so I can stay.

Remembering the times in the basement, smelling of incense and weed, the walls are covered with paintings, photos, and sketches. They were scribble compared to what I've seen tonight. The basement was warm and dimly lit. The whole vibe down there was totally opposite the jerk at the store. Anthony is truly unique.

I remembered him being very hospitable as offered me something to drink and told me to make myself at home on the couch. It was positioned not too far from his bed. He didn't have a television. His continuous reggae jazz played softly.

"I want to paint you."

So deep in thought, when I look around, I can't remember how I got this close to my apartment so quickly.

"No. I don't know you like that."

"People get their portraits painted all the time from artist they don't know. They just want a nice portrait."

I watched him roll his joint. He is the definition of cool. All his wild stories, crazy humor, and the love of his craft had me intrigued for real, but I thought all he was after were my panties; hence the continuous arguing.

"You can't paint me."

It wasn't long after the Frederick fiasco that I decided to let Anthony paint a portrait of me. It was the spell. It's like I can tell Anthony no but sooner or later I always give in.

I'm finally home. I check the mirror before getting out of the car. It's eleven thirty five. I got my story together just in case Chris wants to ask a few questions.

Opening the door quietly, like a burglar breaking into my own home. I can see only the light from the television. Chris is still on the couch where I left him sound asleep. Tipping upstairs, making it to the bedroom safely without a sound. I drop my purse and keys on the bed. I check Manasha's room. The sight of the kids lying all over each other with Brownie right in the middle is a Kodak moment. I wish I had a camera.

In the dimly lit basement, Anthony positioned me in a provocative manner. I straddled a chair with a long red sheet wrapped around my naked body. He told me I would have to sit in that position for three hours at least two days a week for three weeks. I agreed, only if he kept this portrait our secret. Absolutely no one could know about our meetings. If I thought someone knew about it, the deal was off.

For the next three weeks, Anthony was a professional. He was quiet and focused. Never wasting a moment on anything trivial he was in a zone. I didn't know how to focus. His scent throws me off. Twitching in my seat, hungry, my phone distracting me not to mention the many times I had to pee. He smoked marijuana and was focused like a surgeon with a scalpel.

Each meeting, I was getting more comfortable and relaxed. It was only when he had to reposition me that the tension seemed uneasy.

My reflections come alive as I lay in my bed. I can feel my body heating up rapidly.

Miss Kim

The last day of the painting Anthony gave in to my temptations. When placing the sheet strategically over my breast, he touched me slightly. His touch merged with his scent forced my body into his wanting him to take me at that moment. It had to happen because I wanted it to. I can feel him touching me all over again. He didn't say a word. He picked me up laid me on his bed, took his clean paintbrush, and stroked my entire body. He liked watching my body shake and squirm when he tickled in all the right places. Then he'd bury his face deep into my moist abyss. I want him now.

That's why I went to the opening to prove to myself that I am truly in love with my fiancé. So if I am, why did I make that call? Why did I stay? Why did I let him put his arms around me? Why am I touching myself right now at the thought of another man kissing me slow?

Instantly I spring up straight in my bed. I got stop this. What we shared is over, or is it?

Miss Kim

Tomorrow is the last rehearsal. In two weeks, I will be Mrs. Christian Daniel Mitchell.

Nothing is going according to schedule. Chris is still working on his last project, being very evasive about what he's working on. The project is working him late into the evenings. Some days, I don't see or talk him.

That was ok because I am busy trying to find a bank to lend me money for my store. I don't have time to be angry with him for his delinquent behavior. He's working.

None of the banks are willing to take a chance on me, but I know who will.

I call Brock Davidson. He and William did combine their companies and is now President and Vice President of <u>Griffen and Brock Computers</u> of Augusta, Georgia.

I explain to them my plans and predictions of revenue on a conference call. Without hesitation, they agree to help me with my endeavors. Whatever I need, they are at my disposal. They want to know why I didn't come to them first. We are meeting up at the hotel near the airport. We haven't seen each other since the conference; they are only here for one night. That's when we will sign a contract and discuss the plans.

That night they both have gifts for me because they will not be attending my nuptials on account of business. Once again, the threesome are back together painting the town for one night only. We partied hard just like old times. They ask me about Mrs. Cheryl.

"No, I haven't seen her but I got a feeling I will."

"What happened? I thought ya'll was cool.

Everything seemed ok when we were at the conference. I never did understand the whole thing."

"Well actually, me and Mrs. Cheryl were more than just friends, but she took it to a level I wasn't on. I was just having a little fun, you know, like *we* had fun."

I knew once I said something about that night they would jump on it.

"You know we can have an encore anytime you want right?" Brock reminds me.

"You both know I'm getting married right?"

I give them both a kiss on the cheek before they board their plane.

The two men look at each other briefly, "Soooo do you want your *last* encore on the plane or what?"

*E*veryone is waiting patiently for Chris to arrive at the church for the last rehearsal. He is an hour late. We are waiting for him.

Mrs. Claudine, my mother who is on my nerves wants me to start the rehearsal without him. She says she will go over everything with him when he gets here. My nerves are beginning to fray a little.

"Here Dani, a couple outside told me to give this to you and your husband to be. They were in a rush but wanted me to pass this gift to you."

Mrs. Vanderpool gives me a wonderfully wrapped box.

"The woman said for you to open it now. You may need it. They were in a black Tahoe truck. The woman said she would catch up to you later."

The rehearsal stops for a moment, so I can take a quick gander inside. There were documents with a large amount of money in the box. I skim the documents quickly. I read the part naming me part beneficiary of $50,000. It seems I inherited some of the insurance money from the explosion.

I am ecstatic, confused, yet ecstatic. I dance around the church and praise the Lord for his abundant love. I'm so stirred up I share my newfound wealth with all those in my rehearsal. I make an extra large contribution to the church. All in the sanctuary shouts for joy.

This money combined with the money that Brock and William gave me is more than enough to do all I planned. I just fell to my knees and cried, "Thank You Jesus."

Later on that evening when Chris and I were talking about the money, we went through the paperwork and it stated me as a beneficiary of $50,000 if the store was ruled accidental. We figured the insurance company must have paid her also.

Chris asked me, did I know she named me beneficiary on her policy and why not her husband?

I really didn't know what to say. I didn't know anything about her business as far as who was receiving what. She never discussed anything like that with me.

"Maybe she didn't want her husband to have the money. I told you about their marriage. Maybe that was her way of getting back at him for treating her the way he does. I don't know."

At Stephani's House

The gifts are stacked neatly on the well-arranged table. All the jams are playing throughout the game room of Stephani's house. It's my bachelorette party.

"Stephani, where the strippers at?"

I am feeling real good after two gin and cranberry drinks. All the ladies from my family and friends are having a wonderful time sipping, mingling, and cackling like hens.

"I didn't invite any strippers tramp. This is going to be a dignified party, thank you."

"You are act more and more like your mother everyday. You better watch it."

Sakoya is here with me celebrating. We both can't stop smiling, full of liquor and joy.

"Let's call Chris and see what he doing at his bachelor party."

"Let's not. Who is that chick named Veronica?"

"Well, it is James' off and on girlfriend. The mother of his two kids; Myles and Jessica. I needed someone else for the bridal party. You and Nadine are my only two good friends. I asked her. I figure we might as well start getting acquainted, especially since her kids had spent plenty of time at the apartment. She seems all right."

I hear Stephani's phone ring. "Is it the strippers?" I ask.

"Hmm huh. Hmm huh. Yeah...ok Hmm huh. Bye," Stephani hangs up the phone, "Time to open the gifts." Stephani gathers the intimate circle of women around me. I start opening my sister's gift first.

"Dani, this is for you. I didn't know what to get you. I shouldn't have to get you anything because I'm throwing this lavish party. Since you are my baby sister, I decided to get you something you will need."

"See that's something mama would say."

I get this huge box handed to me. Sakoya comes and sits right next to me peering over to see what Stephani has given. I open the box slowly, pulling out many thick, colorful decorative bath towels.

"Thank you Stephani. You can never have too many towels."

My next gift is from Sakoya, "Hurry up."

She is eager to see my reaction. In her box is a spaghetti strap, black see through teddy, with thong, robe, and stockings. I hold it close to my body and model it for the others to see. They knew what I was going to do in that teddy. I received a loud applause for my cat walk with lingerie dangling from my chest.

I get this small box next. I tried to guess but tight lipped Stephani won't tell me. It's a set of keys and a blindfold with a note in the box.

"These keys will open the future for you. If you wish to unlock your future, cover your eyes and make a wish."

"What? What is this all about? Do these keys unlock the door to the strippers?"

The ladies make me sit down to cover my eyes, give me the keys, and tell me to hold on to them.

I'm sitting in the middle of the room with a blindfold on, hearing all kinds of shuffling about, snickering, and I think someone farted.

Stephani makes sure the blindfold is still in place, "Do you have the keys?"

"Yes. What are we doing, and where are we going?" I'm getting anxious.

"Just hold on to me."

I decide, since I'm the one being carted off like a slave in the dark, that I'm going ask question after question until someone breaks. Stephani is sitting next to me in the back seat.

"Who's driving?"

"Does it matter? Just shut up and ride. You giving me a headache."

"Well, if you had gotten the strippers like I told you, I wouldn't be getting on your nerves."

Everyone in the car is laughing.

After a while the car finally stops. I hear other car doors slamming shut.

"Ya'll takin' me to the strip club?"

"No girl, be still and watch your head. Do you still have the keys?"

"Yes, yes here they are."

"Ok, here we go..."

Stephani removes the mask from my eyes. It takes a minute for me to focus.

We are all standing in front of a new building. A building recently built from the ashes of what used to be Reed's Greeting Card store. The new building has a new name. The same name she told her brother-in-law she would one day name her store, Dani's Cards and More.

There I am standing in front of my dream. My vision has come to life. I have no words. I just start jumping for joy. All the ladies are clapping, screaming, and jumping with me.

"Oh my God! Oh my God! Oh my God!"

"C'mon...You have to use your keys." My sister tells me.

I walk arm in arm with my sister across the street.

"Oh my God!" My shivering hands cover my mouth.

The women crowd around me as I stick my key in the brand-new shiny lock.

It didn't work. I try the other key, and it unlocks. We step in. The lights come on.

"Surprise!" Chris, Calvin, Mr. Thompson, James, Kyle, Brandon, Lawrence, Myles, Uncle Blu, Quentin, and Rev. Booker all blurt out in their own way.

I jump back.

Chris comes and stands in front of me. "Hey *peanut*. Happy Bachelorette Day."

I jump in his arms. My tears start falling.

"Aaaawww," Every one in the room feels the love.

"This is why I have been so late coming home. I couldn't wait to show you. You like it? It's yours!"

"I love it."

Veronica locks the door and closes the blinds. The music starts, Stephani and the women uncover a plethora of food. Ribs, chicken, steak, ham, turkey, macaroni and cheese, collard greens, mustard greens, candied yams, green beans, cornbread, and German chocolate cake.

There's a tap on the door. I open the door to my store for the first time. It's Mrs. Claudine walking in holding my favorite, sweet potato pie. Mrs. Belinda Mitchell, Mrs. B., Manasha, and Jessica all follow Mrs. Claudine to the counter. They all kiss and congratulate me on the way in.

Rev. Booker gathers everyone to hold hands and form a circle. Rev. Booker gives thanks to the Lord for the nourishing food. He asks that many blessings rain down on the new store and the people here in the store. We all say "Amen".

"'Scuse me. Where are the strippers?" Mrs. B. wants to know.

Miss Kim

The next day is wash my daughter's hair day, another job in itself. I want to send her to the salon with a packed lunch so I won't have to bother with it. But it's my bonding time with my daughter. I find out a lot things about her. She talks so much and tells everything she knows. I find out things about the whole family actually.

We are having our typical bonding time. Nasha's screaming because she doesn't want soap in her eyes, however, her hair isn't wet yet. I have to tussle with her to lie flat so I can start, but she wants to put her hands in the water, look at the water, splash the water, and everything except put her hair under the water. Good times.

My phone rings, "Hello." I should have looked to see who it is before answering.

"He..Hello Dani. How are you? It's great to hear your voice again. How have you been? I really didn't think you would answer. I thought I would get your voicemail."Frederick St. James is on the other end.

"What do you want? Why are you calling me?"

"Please give me a chance to explain…"

"Explain what?"

"Why I did what I did."

"I could care less why you did what you did!"

I step out of the kitchen so my daughter can't hear me.

"Dani, you have a right to be angry. I've called you on several occasions to apologize. Hear me out please."He's begging at this point.

"Hello. Are you still there?"

"No. I'm not!" I slam the phone down.

It rings again.

"Hello. Stop calling me I don't have anything to say to you. I don't want to hear anything you have to say so get off my phone."

"I know where you live I can come by and maybe we talk please? I know you're getting married and all that, but I have to talk to you before you do that, just hear me out. I love you Dani. I always have. They made me…"

I hang up again and turn down the volume on the phone.

I cannot believe this is happening. This is my luck though. Every time I'm happy something always happens to try and spoil it. My mother would say that's when the devil shows up to spoil all that is good. I understand now.

Chris is good. The closer we get to our wedding date the more the devil shows up trying to keep me from doing what the Lord loves, marriage. I feel like I'm being tempted every day.

First, Anthony and his whole new change, his vibe, the mural of me on his office wall was too enticing for me. He loves me, and I saw proof of it all over his walls. He's always wanted us to be together but I just couldn't. He didn't seem like the marrying type. After seeing him the other night at *his* art opening, a great man has emerged from those ashes of the store into something great.

Then my encounter with my "special friends" William and Brock, with whom I've formed a partnership deemed the WDBC, came to help me with no questions asked. They are doing well for themselves and didn't hesitate to help me. That is what our pledge is all about, but will my husband to be under our friendship?

No. I can hear him now, "How ya'll

become so close?"

Then I will have to lie because he definitely will not understand that I have slept with both of them at the same time on *two* occasions.

"What's this WDBC about? If y'all so close why did one of them try to kill you?"

This brings me to Mrs. Cheryl my boss, the C in WDBC, my mentor, my friend and occasional lat night erotic fetish partner of three years tried to kill me in a greeting card store explosion. She wants more of an exclusive relationship with me, but I don't want that at all. I was experimenting, having a great time that's all. I had no idea it would turn into something like attempted murder! They haven't found her or her husband yet.

Now this stupid phone call is the straw that will try and break my back.

"Mommy, are you going to finish my hair?"

The sound of my daughter's voice brings me back to reality. I'm getting married and nothing or no one will stand in my way. I do love Chris. He is the best thing that has ever happened to me. I never felt this way before. I want to become a better person when I think of him. Watching him with his mother and family, I know he will be a great father to my child and our children. The work ethic he shows is unrelenting and the finished product is always eyebrow raising and incredible; he is ingenious. He will be my husband.

"Mommy, somebody is at the door! What's the matter with you?"

"Oh my God! Why Jesus? Why me! This cannot be happing."

"I told you I want to talk," says Frederick.

"Frederick, get away from me or I will call the police!"

"*Dearly* Beloved..."

Looking into his eyes, I can't believe it's finally happening. We're standing before the Pastor I've known all of my life. In the church I grew up in mentally and spiritually.

"We gather here today to join this man and this woman in Holy Matrimony," Rev. Booker pauses for dramatic effect.

My body is trembling. My hands are sweating profusely, and I have to pee. I made sure I went before walking down the isle and then a thousand times before that. I'm going to lose my balance, fall, and lose my water right here, right now.

Chris tightens his grip of our hands. It's like he knows I'm over here freaking out. He looks directly into my eyes to keep my focus on him then he breathes in deeply, so do I. I feel more at ease.

"I believe these two have written their own vows," Rev. Booker took an inch step back.

Chris looks me in my eyes again then speaks,"Danielle *peanut* Thompson, on this day I pledge to you my heart, my soul. I never thought I'd meet or marry someone as beautiful, intelligent, and sweet as you. You have taught me a lot about love and life. The lessons I've learned have changed my heart. You will be more than just my wife. You're the blood in my veins, and the air I breathe. If I were suddenly blind, your beautiful face I can still see. My heart beats for you and only you. I want to be every man for you whatever, whenever; however 'til death do us part."

"Amen" echoes over the church quietly.

My throat clogs up with a gigantic lump. He's talking about me! The tears are coming fast. I try to hold them back but I can't. I blot with my small lace handkerchief, hidden discreetly in my palm. I can't believe I affect this man like this. He is saying so many wonderful things. I hear a little voice say, *I deserve them.*

I'm now taking several deep breaths because I'm full with his total sincerity. Feeling his love flowing through each and every word, "the blood in his veins," wow, that's deep. He smiles at me and the butterflies dance around in my stomach. I want to kiss him now.

Rev. Booker turned his attention to me. It's my turn to speak. This is it. My nerves are getting the best of me because I know my words aren't quite as elegant as his are to me, "Christian, I am blessed again today with yet another life changing miracle in my life, you. The day he placed you in my life he knew there would be change, for the both of us. Being with you has opened my eyes to a happier tomorrow. I am fortunate to never have to walk alone again. You are my strength when I am weak; my voice when I cannot speak. I know we will build an incredible life together, and I thank God for you everyday. I will love, honor, and cherish our love and life together from this day on. I love you."

Amen again, there wasn't a dry eye in the church.

Chris is smiling and crying at the same time, so of course I start too. But I don't want to ruin my makeup, so I try to stop immediately. No one wants to shake hands with a crybaby bride with running black eye liner and mascara looking like a raccoon caught in the headlights.

The Reverend steps up to the mic. The service is interrupted by a barrage of police sirens right outside the church. The sirens stopped abruptly.

"Do you Danielle Nicole Thompson take this man to be your lawfully wedded husband?"

"I do."

The butterflies are shouting at this point, and I really have to pee now.

"Do you Christian Daniel Mitchell take this woman to be your lawfully wedded wife?"

Chris clears his throat first. He must have a lump too.

"I do."

"Is there any one here showing just cause why these two should not bond together in Holy matrimony? Speak now or forever hold your peace."

Rev. Booker extends his hand toward the congregation. There is a little movement in the congregation. A gentleman stands in the middle section of the sanctuary. We can barely see him standing in the far middle section. The glare from the sunlight blocks our vision. We can tell everyone else's attention is focused on the man standing. The church is still. My heart is racing.

I can see it's Anthony scooting through the people sitting on the pew. He walks out of the church quietly. Everyone watches him leave.

I keep my eyes on Chris. My lump is back. I'm feeling a little anxiety at this point because I want to know what my husband thinks about what just happened.

"Rev. Booker, I do have something to say."

The congregation turns around to see Frederick St. James is standing, waiting to speak. His wife sits next to him, by the look on her face, she is not pleased at all with whatever her husband is doing.

"I… I… I just want to say to Dani I'm sorry for all the trouble I caused some years ago. I want the congregation to know you had every right to lash out the way you did that Sunday. I never meant to hurt you; you look so beautiful. Chris you are marrying a wonderful woman. I bid you all the best. You belong together. I'm sorry Rev. you may continue."

Frederick is clearly upset as he takes his seat. The attention is immediately directed back to us.

"I now pronounce you husband and wife."

The whole sanctuary stands to their feet cheering and clapping with thunderous applause.

"You may now kiss…"

Before Rev. Booker finishes his sentence, we were already kissing. The applause starts again.

"That was a beautiful service. I did a wonderful job. Don't you think? I wonder what that guy wanted to say. He sure got outta there quick," Chris is teasing.

I know he's asking me without asking directly.

"Hey, what's going on over there?"

The well-wishers form a path for us to pass through on the way to our limousine. Holding hands, Chris and I walk quickly through the crowd. We can see there are many police cars right outside of the doors of the church. I thought maybe something was going on across the street. It's always something over there.

"Thank you so much…"

We are waving to our cheering family and friends, when two officers approach us.

"Miss Danielle Thompson," The officer

grabs my arm.

"You have the right to remain silent..."

"What? This all a mistake...Oh my God!"

"What!! What's going on?!" Chris yells at the second police officer.

"I'm sorry. Your wife is under arrest for conspiracy to commit murder, the murder of Nadine Abigail Hughes.

Everyone is looking at me sitting in the back of the police cruiser. Reading their faces, I can see they don't understand because I don't understand. Nadine was my friend. I would never do anything to hurt her. This is all a big huge mistake, but they didn't have to ruin my wedding day like this. They could have waited one more day or even the day before. On my wedding day, who authorized that?

My parents are yelling that they will be right behind me. They will get me out.

When the cruiser door closes on my wedding gown, that's when I lose it. I hang my head low. Chris runs to the window pressing his hand to the glass.

"Don't worry baby. I'll get you out. I love you."

A black truck drives by slowly as the cruiser is taking off. The tinted windows, rolled down slightly, low enough for me to see her signature black cat sunglasses, Mrs. Cheryl blew me a kiss as she rode by grinning.

"Stop that truck! She's in there! Stop that..."

"Pipe down back there. You need to be concerned about what's happening to you right now."

"She is the reason why I'm back here *right now* dammit and she's getting away! Cheryl Reed is in that truck! Stop her!"

I am screaming at the top of my lungs with my hands cuffed behind my back. She's right in front of their eyes, and they are just sitting here letting the bitch get away. So I just start kicking the divider gate having a true hissy-fit in the backseat. I figure I deserve to have a fit right now. After all that has happened and it isn't over yet, not to mention I'm in my wedding gown!

We take off headed in the opposite way of the black truck. I did hear the officer page the officers behind him to follow the truck. We're going downtown.

After the whole uncomfortable search, I' m taken to the interrogation room immediately. The police are acting as if they've really caught the person who killed Nadine.

"State your name."

"Danielle Thompson."

"You mean Mitchell. Congratulations by the way, your wedding dress is beautiful. I'm Officer Peterson."

I remember the attractive officer. He was sitting outside Nadine's room the night me and Nasha went to visit her. He must be the good cop.

"Well, Officer Peterson if you know, why did you ask? Thank you for destroying what was supposed to be the best day of my life. You have the wrong person. You let the murderer get away! When this is all over, and you find I had nothing to do with Nadine's murder, the whole police precinct will pay."

A police officer is the first person to say my new married name back to me. This will be forever etched in my mind.

"Before you sue us Mrs. Mitchell, we have

reason to believe you are indeed involved in Nadine Hughes' murder. How well did you know your boss Mrs. Cheryl?"

"She hired me about three years ago. Kinda took me under her wing and showed me the ins and outs of owning a small business. We were friends also."

"How close were you?" The other officer weighed in.

I've never seen this officer before. He looks like he hasn't missed a doughnut in years. He's playing the bad cop.

"We're good friends and co workers. Well, you could say she was my mentor that's all."

"Mrs. Mitchell, you need to be totally honest with us. You are facing serious charges, and if you don't cooperate, we will send you straight to jail today in your wedding gown. Now tell us how close are you and Mrs. Reed?"

"Like I said we worked together and were close friends."

"Okay. Let's try a different route... Why would your boss want to kill Nadine Hughes?"

"My boss did not want to kill Nadine Hughes."

"How are you so sure?"

"Because Nadine was covering for me that day."

"Covering for you..."

"Mrs. Cheryl asked me to come in early on both Friday and Saturday because she was going on a business trip and the water meter man was coming early around six thirty. She wouldn't be back until Sunday. I agreed but I had a doctor's appt Friday morning at seven, so I ask Nadine to work for me until I got there."

"So you knew Mrs. Reed was going out of town, and you asked the deceased to cover for you while you were at the doctor's office, right? Write down the name and number of the doctor please."

The questioning officer took that piece of paper immediately out of the room. Officer Peterson continues his interrogation.

"Did you know your boss was planning to commit this crime on that particular day? Is that why you switched shifts? You and Mrs. Cheryl planned the entire thing."

"Why would I do that officer? This is ridiculous! Why would I want to kill one of my best friends?"

"Did you or did you not receive payment for your part in the murder?"

"No, I did not receive payment."

"We have reason to believe on the night of your wedding rehearsal you received an undisclosed amount of money. That was the payment. If I'm correct that money came with papers stating you were a benefiary in case of accidental fire, correct?"

"I have no idea where that money came
from. Someone gave it to me as a gift for our wedding. That's all I know about that money."

"How is your husband doing with all this? He's here along with the rest
of your family. Does he know about this too? Is he in on it?"

"Please leave him out of this. No, he is not in on anything because I didn't do anything. I don't care how you twist my words. I did not kill Nadine Hughes. I did not know about anyone setting the store on fire. I don't know anything about payment for a murder. I DON'T KNOW! Let me take a lie detector test."

"Sure we can do that, but be aware that all things come out with these tests you know that right? Like your little extra curricular activities..."

"What are you talking about? I told you I had nothing to do with any of it!"

"You know full well what I'm talking about. We know all about you Mrs. Mitchell, since this investigation, we've had to take a close look at you. We know all about your ongoing fling with Anthony the security guard at the store. Just a couple of weeks ago you met up with two guys you met when you and your boss went to a business convention. You convinced them to give you a large amount of money, is that right? Was that before or after the threesome on their private plane? Seems you're a frequent member of the "Mile High Club.""

Officer Peterson seems to be enjoying himself at my expense. He's walking around me like a shark circling his prey. I'm wrong. He's the bad cop.

"Does your husband know he's married a manipulative, gold digger with no conscience? So before you met him, you and your on again off again freaky lover devised a plan to set the store on fire "accidently" to get the insurance money. She would then leave her husband and you were to meet her at some disclosed destination, isn't that right? But you stabbed Mrs. Cheryl in the back by getting married. She turned on you and tried to kill you, but you switched shifts and she got your friend instead. I'm positive you don't want your husband to know all this."

"Please don't. What do you want me to say? I didn't kill her, and I wasn't in on some kind of plan."

"We are certain that the explosion was caused by a phone call. The explosive was tripped when Nadine answered the phone. We traced all the calls going into the store starting at approximately six o'clock. She received several calls from you on her cell phone, but we traced two calls coming into the store at the same time of the explosion, one signal from your phone and one from an untraceable number, but we were able to trace the location from where the second call was made. It was made from a plane headed to Mexico."

"What does all that mean officer?"

"It means we have to figure out which call killed her or you can help us help you."

Minute by minute my life it seems to be turning to shit. Just when I think it can't get worse it does. It seems the police did hear me when I told them to pick up Mrs. Cheryl. Turns out she is in the next holding cell over. They want me to talk to her and get her to confess to the arson that led to Nadine's death.

This is some kind of nightmare that I cannot rise from. Why am I here? This whole process is for other people, not me. What did I do to deserve this? Well, I'm about to find out from the killer herself. I can't believe the one I shared so much with wants me dead. What am I suppose to say to her? Am I just supposed to walk in there in my mascara stained wedding gown and ask her why she tried to kill me? I have to pee first.

Officer Peterson assures me they are watching, listening, and taping everything. She can't hurt me or get to me. He says, once we have her confession admitting she masterminded the entire thing, then I can go home to my new husband.

"I want to go home."

"Your husband is right outside that door.
All you gotta do is go in there and be yourself.
Don't be afraid. She can't hurt you. She's in one
cell. You will be in the other. Chris can't hear
anything. We've sent your family home only
because we don't know how long this will take.
Don't worry about any of that. We are right outside
the room. She knows that also, okay? Everything
will be fine. Just press those buttons, and she will
talk. By the way, you make a beautiful bride, and
your dress is awesome."

"Thank you, and you told me that already."

After my third trip to the bathroom, I
thought I was ready. My whole body is shaking
uncontrollably. I want to throw up.

"Please be with me Jesus as I walk through
the valley of the shadow of death. I will fear no
evil."

The guards open the cell next to Mrs.
Cheryl. She looks good like always. I don't know
what I expected, a monster or something hideous,
but it's Mrs. Cheryl, my girlfriend.

"Wow, you still got on your wedding dress?
It's beautiful."

"Why did you try to kill me!"

"Why did you throw me away like
yesterday's trash!"

"Are you serious? Grow up! You blaming
me for things I had nothing to do with? You
became attached to me because your marriage
wasn't working. You know David's never going to
divorce you. Not only will he not divorce you, he's
only staying with you to torture you because he
blames you for his paralysis. You're estranged

from your only child, and your brother won't forgive you for saving your own life. So when you met me, you already had problems.

I told you from the start we were only friends, good friends. You acted as if you were cool with it. Had I known you were going to take it so serious, serious enough to try and kill me, I would have never let you…"

"Never let me… What you mean? Every time I called you came running."

"That's because you always had some kind of melt down just to get me over there, so that's why you tried to kill me?"

"No, I didn't try to kill you. I know what you trying to do. I know they got you in here hoping I'm going to say something to incriminate myself, but guess what honey they don't have anything on either one of us. What that detective told you was all circumstantial. They can't prove anything, so when you leave today, I leave today. We are in this together."

"No, we are not! Why are you doing this?"

"Yeah, you're right. I did have problems before I met you. I told you all about them and yet you still dogged me. How could you be so heartless? You know how vulnerable and weak I am. You know I need you in my life. I did everything for you! Who did you call when you wrecked your car over Frederick? Me! I bought new clothes for you so you could fit in at the conferences. I bought the damn diamond earrings you wear every day. But what did you do? Screwed two men in front of me, screwed me, had everyone fall in love with you. Then, when we came back, you treat me like shit in my own store. What can I do, I'm in love with you Dani. You stirred feelings in me I didn't even know I had. Don't you remember?

You have no idea how you affect people. There is something about you that draws people in, and we all want to be apart of your life, but you're so selfish you can't even see it. You don't think Anthony wanted to stop your wedding when he just suddenly left at that particular time? He's loved you the first day he saw you. He told me. He knew you were out of his league, but he vowed to keep trying until you came around and you did. It was the night I sent you over there to take him his check. We set it up. Of course, I had no interest in you then.

Out of nowhere Frederick stands to apologize to you for your temporary insanity during church service because he was seeing both you and Chloe. Frederick got Chloe pregnant, her father, Reverend Booker made him marry her and take a job as the Pastor of his own church in Tennessee. Now he and his wife are going through a divorce, and he realizes he should have never left you, but it's too late. So he made that pathetic speech in front of everyone, embarrassing his wife, your new husband, and himself all for you on your wedding day."Mrs. Cheryl is in tears.

"Were you in the church?"I was puzzled.

"You have no remorse do you? You could careless how deeply these people feel about you. It's not your fault. You and your sister were raised that way. The both of you have been given everything in life. That's why you don't value what you have. Tell me how *is* your sister doing these days?"

"Why are you talking about my sister? You don't know her like that?"

"You would be surprised who I know. Did she make a full recovery? I remember Brandon being devastated when he found out his wife had an affair. Does it run in your family or something?"

"Whatever. Look, just stay away from me and my family. It's over."I'm of hearing her ramble on and on.

"It's over when I say it's over, and I'm just getting started! See, I'm running this now. Before I let you push me around, because I wanted you so bad, but now I'm in control. IT AIN'T OVER!

Your selfish ass sister got what she wanted and deserved too! Yeah my father and I talked about it. She learned her lesson now it's time for you to learn."

"What do you want from me? Wait a minute…What did you say?"

"I don't want anything from you. You don't have shit I don't already have three times over. I just want you. Don't you want to take our love to the next level?"

"No, I don't. I am married now, okay. I'm sorry, but I'm in love with my husband!"

"We will see how much he's in love with you when you tell him about me. Trust me, when he finds out you have been lying to him all this time, your marriage will be over before it begins. He doesn't love you! He doesn't even know you!"

"What?"

"You heard me. Tell him about me and everything else."

"I already told him about you."

"No, you didn't. So you told him how you liked it when I gave it to you on the plane, in my office, in my truck… You didn't tell him the real truth."

"What's the real truth Cheryl?"

"We are in love."

"I am not in love with you! You are a sick individual. Why are you trying to destroy my life?"

"Because you and your family destroyed mine. You played Russian Roulette when you messed with me and mine, so I'm about to pull the trigger! Guards please bring Mr. Mitchell in."

When I hear the door open, and his footsteps slowly coming closer, I'm suddenly paralyzed. I cannot wake up from this hellish nightmare. He's standing in front of me in his tux waiting for me to say something, something that may ease his mind of the horrid events that have occurred today. In his eyes, I see love and kindness overshadowed by doubt and fear. This is it.

"You ready to go baby?" Chris hugs me so tight.

"Oh before you go Chris your new bride has something she wants to tell you." Mrs. Cheryl yelled from the cell.

We sit in that jail cell for what seems like an eternity. Chris, Mrs. Cheryl, and the whole police department listen to me as I confess to my new husband of one day, all my sins. I stutter, cry, and try to explain my less than angelic past. Chris just sits there looking at me with a stone cold expression. As I explain the WDBC, our encounter in the bungalow, his emotions got the best of him. Each glare from Chris pierces me like the sharpest knife. The same knife digs deeper when Cheryl speaks out from the other cell.

"Tell how they just *gave* you money for your store. Money she doesn't need because you took care of everything and built it for her. Ask her about that transaction."

Suddenly the chair he is sitting in flies across the room. It's all too much for him. How can anyone process so much damaging information at one time?

Chris stands to his feet and walks out the precinct without looking back.

"Are you happy now? It's over. Guards please let me out of here."

The guard opens the door.

"Oh yeah, before you go love, could you do me a favor?"

"Fuck you Cheryl!"

"Whenever you're ready. Until then tell my little brother hello.

"What?"

"Oh, don't you know? We are kinda related, but not really, so we can still kick it like we do. Lawrence is *my* little brother. I can't wait to meet him. Tell Stephani daddy sends his love. See it won't ever be over 'til you come back to me. I will be waiting."

When I finally get out of jail, I don't see Chris anywhere. I can't blame him for not sticking around. In my heart, I want him to be here. I want him to say he forgives me, but I know this is wishful thinking. How can he forgive me for lying to him from the beginning?

Walking down the jailhouse steps at five o'clock in the morning, the street is bare. Nothing is moving. The sun is just peeking over the clouds. Starting out on my walking journey I take a deep breath and head out. A black familiar truck pulls up beside me slowly.

"Can I give you a ride?" Chris gets out of his truck and helps me in on the passenger side, being careful not to close my wedding gown in the door.

Once back in the truck, my husband of two days turns to me, looks me square in the eye and repeats, "Do you promise to love and cherish me through sickness and health forsaking all others keeping yourself only to me and only me 'til death do us part?"

"I do."

About the Author

My name is Kim Kendall. When I started writing Sweatin', I was pregnant with my son, Avien. I was off from work with time on my hands. I hadn't written anything since high school. I wrote the first page and immediately became excited. I wanted to write something that was fun, suspenseful, and daring.

Many of the instances in Sweatin' are stories I have collected while serving in the Military as a cook. It was plenty gossip in the hair salon I worked in briefly. Both the stylist and the customers never seem to let me down when it came to the "juicy details."

A short stint in an office cubical, and a long tenure in a car plant proved to be all the information I needed to write an erotic, suspense filled drama. Equipped with my own imagination and creativity, I started writing.

The more I wrote the more the characters came alive with their own personalities and agendas.

Miss Kim

AMB

K BOOKS

Miss Kim

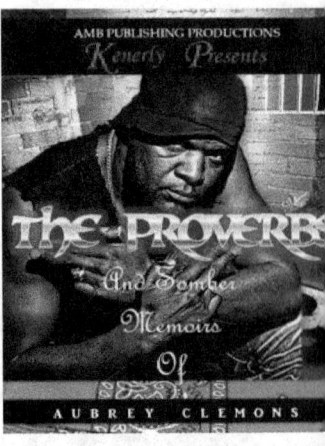

www.ingramcontent.com/pod-product-compliance
Lightning Source LLC
Chambersburg PA
CBHW070553130626
46556CB00001B/136